KISSING DARKNESS

DARK SPELL SERIES BOOK 2

ISRA SRAVENHEART

To James. Thank you for being a good and kind friend to me. For helping me hold it together in staying positive even at times where I wanted to give it all up in favor of something less fulfilling that would ultimately have bored me to tears. I knew you wanted to be in this from the very beginning. And how could I possibly deny that?

You are as real as your fictional counterpart, and more importantly you've played a role in things that neither of us can inexplicably understand, but it's all part of the process. It's why I had no doubt about you.

Mr. Salty. While I admit it is true that you drove me absolutely bonkers with the why and wherefore and your reasoning, you made me see things as they are. And for that, I thank you. You are my grounding element. You keep me rooted in this earth like nobody else can.

1

_____

Samuel rushed into his office clutching a lukewarm mug of coffee in his left hand. The man had already experienced a chaotic morning, having the metaphysical chimes practically ringing in his ears from those "on high," but the light bringer was exhausted. Just imagine his surprise, thinking he was alone only to be met by the solemn glance of Astrid.

"Ah boy, I wondered where you were. Do you like slightly warm coffee? I can't say I recommend it too highly," Samuel chirped, grimacing as he took a sip.

"I'm not here for the sanctimonious refreshments, Samuel," Astrid countered, clearly pissed at Samuel.

But why he was upset, Samuel had no inclination of. Could it be that the dear friend of Astrid had offended the poor raven, or did he have his feathers in a twist over something else? Or perhaps _someone_ ... a certain femme fatale he was rather fond of? Well, it could be that.

"Yes well, I'd rather have a fresh one, but there's just no time, you know? So much to do," Samuel jested, swigging the rest of the coffee that was now stone cold. "That is vile, indeed!" The light bringer spluttered, pulling a face of disgust as he looked upon the raven favorably. "So do tell me. What brings you here in such a dander, hmm? It's not your time of the month, is it?"

Samuel noted the raven was situated a little farther away from him than usual today. *How strange. He's normally so chatty. I typically cannot get the bastard to shut up.* Samuel motioned to himself in thought as he realized Astrid's temperament was very different this morning. Slightly brasher than usual.

"Actually, I've just come back from witnessing Isra give up her heart to darkness," Astrid replied, clearly not beating around the bush. His tone was icy but yet pungent as if surrounded by ferocious flames that were not about to cease any time soon.

"Oh. That," Samuel murmured. "Do tell me, what is going on? I'm afraid I'm a little out of the loop."

Astrid resisted the urge to throw out a sarcastic comeback, having already been told to steer clear of Isra more times than he cared to count. But Samuel was clearly unaware and wasn't about to discipline the raven for filling in the blanks, or at least that was how Astrid hoped it would be.

Never mind, he knows nothing. I'm the guy who gets told in no uncertain terms to get out of there and yet they don't know a damn thing. Utterly ridiculous, Astrid thought quietly to himself, regarding how the "on high" was dealing with the intrepid situation.

"Isra and her foe Everilda are at war with each other," Astrid began in a stern tone. "I have witnessed it for myself. Isra is vengeful and out for blood whereas her opponent—" Astrid stopped mid-speech for fear that whatever he said now would get him into a lot of hot water. After all, he wasn't supposed to be within claw's distance from the witch.

But evidently, Samuel had no clue of what was occurring, so better to say what needed to be said now than later, right? What was the worst that could emerge from such a thing? Astrid doubted not much, as he'd already caught sight of enough tormenting things already.

"Everilda," Astrid continued, "was a witch but now is mortal thanks to the gracious folk over at Wingdom's who saw to it."

Samuel almost spat in horrendous shock. "You have to be joking, surely? You mean to tell me that our witch has a foe that is now mortal? Ordained by the very academy we've had our eyes on for months?! Where the fuck is James?" Samuel shouted in frustration, banging his fists upon his desk. "Oh no, this is too much for a morning. I need a shot of whiskey. I can't handle this!"

Samuel snapped, reaching for his decanter eagerly. "And why did the 'on high' not tell us?" he quizzed the raven with a forewarning glance.

"That I do not know. But it's sure to get a lot messier from here on out," Astrid predicted in a somber tone.

"Touché. I must get in touch with James immediately. Someone needs to go down there, assuming she's still out there causing all manner of havoc," Samuel muttered, almost cursing to himself as if he should have been on the ball. He should have been the first to intervene the very second Isra switched from light to dark.

I should have fucking been there. I've been following this woman since we first heard about her existence as well as that energy that was surging through her, sending ripples across the earth as she walked in desolate desperation. I've been reprimanding Astrid for being within arm's length of her and here she turns the tide and I'm not even in the vicinity to do something about it? Oh, I'm an absolute fool! Samuel clashed back and forth with himself.

"Why James?" Astrid asked in a low voice, although there was some kind of irritation that Samuel detected in Astrid's tone.

You could just tell that Astrid really resented James in some form of another. The way he spoke regarding James was callous as though he'd rather James wasn't there because the way Astrid saw it, James was treading upon his carefully raked soil. Astrid did not feel very appeased to that.

He'd already threatened to peck James's eyeballs out once, and perhaps if there wasn't some moral justification from Samuel as a result of taking such extremes, maybe Astrid would have by now. But no, he'd have to sit there and tolerate this human—or whatever James was—being involved as much as Astrid disliked him.

"Because James has experience with witches," Samuel reluctantly came back to Astrid. "He has the know-how and forward planning on how to deal with them in an efficient manner."

"How lovely for him. What a novel way to go about your merry life by dealing with witches, as you so ambivalently put it." Astrid scoffed in a sarcastic yet stroppy tone.

Yet again the raven was indicating he was far from happy to hear of James's involvement with the mission at hand, even though Astrid had no physical ability to intervene in regard to Isra.

"Don't start, boy." Samuel chided the raven with a harsh burning stare, having listened to much of Astrid's ranting already. "The 'on high' has been communicating with me most of the morning. It's gotten pretty rough down there. Perhaps someone should go down personally and intersect with Isra, as apparently things are messy," Samuel added with a furrowed brow.

"Oh, and let me guess, that someone is James?" Astrid snipped back.

He started to preen his feathers, busying himself with that task; almost ignoring Samuel in a sense. It was as though Astrid felt like something vile had tainted his silky black feathers and he was frantically trying to remove it. Perhaps he was just being an ignorant bastard as he suspected Samuel would answer him with, "Yes."

"No!" Samuel responded with a sharp tone.

He veered in closer to the raven, lifting him onto his shoulder so he could speak to him more intently and actually look into Astrid's eyes. This was really the personal touch in Samuel's eyes, the best course of action to get the raven to listen to him for a change.

"You really have no comprehension of what's kicked off, do you? I've heard from my wise associates that Isra hasn't just given up her heart to the dark. No. She's done a bit more than that. I mean, if you had been around her since this morning, you'd have known for yourself just what she has unleashed unto our world."

Samuel spoke in a serious yet withdrawn voice. The light bringer was extremely tired and it had already been a rough start to the day. He had a feeling it was about to get worse. Astrid relented, only giving his master a sympathetic look. After all, Samuel was rather invested in the mission to tease Isra away from the darkness. He didn't look well thinking about it. Samuel looked pale and lifeless in the face. His normal sky-blue eyes that closely resembled the ocean were lackluster and his eyelids puffy. All that coffee had not helped Samuel claim some finesse back from his nonexistent sleep.

Clearly there was more to this mission, this fight against the dark shadowy realms that Samuel was not letting on to. It was something that could only be so deeply painful to make him so embroiled in the life of one witch, fated for something much more gratifying than anyone could have conjured up for her. However, Samuel was not surrendering. He would prevail because this was a lifelong devotion.

It was fickle for anyone, even Astrid, to think that one set-back would cause such a domino effect that would make him give up on a cause he truly believed in. No, Samuel was made of far stronger stuff than to just give in at the first hurdle. He'd play along with Isra, doing things her way if he had to, in order to get her to see the real reasoning of things. If he had to, he'd play dirty. Samuel was no stranger to wicked trickery, especially if it meant he'd overcome the demons by cavorting with them just to make them think they had succeeded in bringing damnation.

Astrid was startled as all of sudden with a glint in his blue eyes, Samuel shifted him off of his shoulder with a concerned look.

"I suppose if there is to be any positive resolution in this, I will have to take this matter into my own hands," the light bringer chirped with a wink, snapping his fingers together as if he had just come up with the plan of a lifetime.

The smile that was just about visible signified that Samuel would indeed find a way.

2

Isra was in a world of her own, in a blissful trance whereby deep concentration was the only concern in her young mind. With all those pathetic, mindless distractions discarded from her person, she stood still on the mountain peak with her eyes closed.

The witch, despite her lack of sleep, looked very much bright eyed and bushy tailed. That was ironic when you considered she had been kept awake all night by the business of her mind. Isra did not look at all exhausted. Her eyes were bright and glossy. An emerald green glow emitting from them that was large enough to light up a whole village indicated that she was much rested in terms of energy, but yet you'd have expected at least one side effect. However, that remains to be seen.

Ignoring the world around her, Isra honed in on her senses feeling the sun's rays collide down her back as she envisioned a shimmery violet light hovering amongst the sunlit cloudless skies. As she maintained her focus, she twisted her hand completely around before blowing into the wide-open air. Now the violet hue was much darker and more prominent, casting a rather murky shade of amethyst. The harsh glare of the blue-violet color was enough to blind anyone who dared look up to the sky.

In a flash, Isra waved her hand clockwise before opening her beguiled lime green eyes just in time to witness a thunderclap cast a shadow upon the glorified land, covering it in a surge of black smoke as something appeared to be visible in the sky. Isra commanded the force of great magnitude by a simple phrase, almost shouting it out as she called, "Oh, thy great one. Come down to me!"

And with that, the deep purple unidentified object was now made clear.

~

"OH, LORD. SHE'S SUMMONED A DRAGON."

Astrid gasped from amongst his secure hiding place in a nearby pine tree. The raven took undue care to ensure he was not seen as he kept his beady eye on the scene before him.

The dragon that Astrid witnessed hovering midair beside Isra was amaranthine but also slightly reddish-blue in his coloring. Astrid could detect it was a male due to the almighty rumbling it made when it admired his surroundings and most importantly, Isra. She was the sole entity who had given him life and a reason to occupy this beautifully dark realm. He was quick in acknowledging Isra with his ruby red eyes.

Being subtle enough to lower his voice, he muttered, "Well, good day. I can only welcome your creation of me with an introduction. Hey, my name is Franco, and you are the most charming soul. Your power is superlative to anything I have witnessed."

"The pleasure is all mine. You are simply irrevocable," Isra predicted with a grin, clearly very impressed with her work.

Watching the majestic creature Franco poised in the air, awaiting whatever instruction she might deliver unto him gave Isra a sense of importance. Finally, she would be listened to by another soul and have some control bestowed upon herself and the life she'd chosen to lead. Although Isra turned away from Franco for a second, she was faced by a tall man with jet black, slicked back hair and soft blue eyes. He was smiling at her for some peculiar reason.

"Oh shit. Samuel!" Astrid realized as he caught sight of the tall light bringer within arm's distance of Isra. *Fuck, I'm not supposed to be here. How on earth did he decide to come down to this part of the world? He certainly didn't discuss it with me,* Astrid rambled in thought as he tried to come up with a plucky plan. He'd have to be quick witted because Samuel was right in front of him about to make a friendly acquaintance with Isra.

Of course, Astrid was strictly forbidden from being anywhere near Isra, so he had to make a fast escape, sharpish before his master realized that yet again Astrid was stalking Isra. And lest we not forget Samuel had already threatened banishment if Astrid were to go against his wishes a second or perhaps a third time. Cunningly the raven turned himself around from his position in the oak tree so he could stay out of Samuel's forewarning eye but yet still keep watch on things. With Samuel here, Astrid was not going anywhere. Oh no, he wanted to see this.

Isra felt slightly unnerved by the man. This bold figure handsomely dressed in fine tailored black overcoat and matching black trousers looked like he wouldn't be out of place from a grand ball at a palace. However, the witch was not impressed with Samuel and so she folded her arms in a defensive stance.

"Who the hell are you?" Isra threw the pressing question at him with a cold, icy rivet.

Samuel almost glared at the witch as he recognized the fiery body language emitting from her in waves, but then he remembered she was someone that was very much entrapped in darkness so he'd have to take a very different modus operandi with her.

"Well, I must say that is rather rude. I am a light bringer. My name is Samuel. I am someone who is seasonally trained in placating holds on dark souls like yourself who have succumbed to the temptation," Samuel explained to her with careful fervor.

Yes, he was powerful in his own unique manner but he wasn't about to offend Isra, for he knew that she'd use any means she possessed to get away from anything that even remotely smelled of the light.

"How nice for you. I bet that's heavenly," Isra retorted with sarcastic flair. She didn't find Samuel's introduction at all attractive. In fact, she found him to be rather overbearing as though he was someone to be feared if you happened to be on the opposite side of the light. *Blahdy blah. I bet he is as dull as he seems!* Isra cajoled in the back of her mind, quietly coming to a resolve that the majestic Samuel was indeed a light bringer as he claimed to be.

"Yes. Anyway ... do you think we can do something about that?" Samuel pointed his index toward Franco in a momentary lapse of comical favor for a second to retain his seriousness on the matter. "You know Isra, you are causing quite a stir down here. We've known about you for a very long time," he added gravely.

"Huh? You *know* about me, how interesting! That's my dragon. His name is Franco," Isra answered, almost snapping at Samuel as she appeared to be very much irritated with him.

"Yes. Well, I am sure he is a wonderful soul, but you know he's a dark being at heart. Dragons are fierce beasts," Samuel commented in a low tone.

However, Isra wasn't going to be swayed by Samuel talking about Franco. It could only be a means to casually distract her as far as she was concerned, and before Samuel could have done anything, Franco swept off into the sky, his long purple wings soaring into the air and then disappearing from civilization.

Isra hadn't even noticed him go off. She was far too preoccupied with the stranger in her presence. Isra was curious. She couldn't help but throw another frosty glare at the light bringer, wondering just how he knew about her and why he was here. Was this some kind of lecture to give her a verbal spanking for the improper use of magic, maybe?

"How do you know my name?" Isra mustered bravely.

Samuel chuckled in her direction. Evidently, he was amused by her question. He cleared his throat a little by coughing before placing his hand across his mouth, excusing himself for his impoliteness. Samuel laughed once more, giving Isra a mischievous smile.

"Oh girl, I know more than just your name. Unrequited love. A friendship broken in two after a betrayal. Darkness tempted you and here we are in the midst of chaos. Now how about you come down from there and we have a nice chat over a cup of coffee back in my realm? We'd have to travel to get there, but I will escort you back exactly how you are if you don't agree with what I have to say. You can continue wreaking havoc if that is your wish, but first you must listen to my reasoning," he commanded in a friendly but yet stalwart tone.

"I am not sure coffee appeals to my unique tastes right now. It's rather bitter," Isra explained in a callous voice as she looked Samuel right in his sky-blue eyes.

"I could endeavor to make it sweeter for you," Samuel suggested.

He placed a finger to his lips as if to pause while he waited to see what Isra would say. He'd thrown it out there. She was welcome to come along with him down to Spirisity if she so deemed it. It was up to her now whether she took him up on it or if she chose to decline his gracious offer.

"Hmm," Isra muttered. "And just exactly what are you going to do if I decide not to come along with you?"

"I had predicted you might respond in such a manner. Very well. Have it your way!" Samuel acknowledged.

He flashed Isra a coy wink. The light bringer was clearly very amused with himself. In an instant he clicked his thumb and index finger together, sending a surge of pure white magic colliding down beside Isra, streaming down by her as she was covered in shimmery white and gold. The energy made haste in surrounding Isra, bringing her down in front of Samuel.

The witch was bemused to find herself standing next to the light bringer who was very pleased with himself judging by the grin that marauded across his face. Samuel then clicked his fingers again. His eyes focused on Isra as he did so. Seconds later, Isra tried in vain to conjure up one of her notoriously deadly lime green orbs, using her hand to attempt to spawn the much-loved entity she had become rather fond of, only for her hand to singe in pain as neither flame nor glow could be found. Isra could only glance at Samuel, flashing him a confused look of defeat, for she could not understand why her action had not generated that which she had sought to create.

Isra gasped in amazement at Samuel with a quizzical stare as she stammered in vain. "But ... but my magic?" Isra faltered. She was unable to take the shock that someone she had just met had well and truly disarmed her with just one simple click of his fingers.

Power was definitely not to be sniffed at in these parts, no matter what form it happened to be in. Those who wielded it and knew exactly how to diligently use it were the ones that had the greatest force. It didn't matter at all whether it was light or dark. And as Isra witnessed Samuel take her own energy if only for a few secret moments, she knew right away that he was one of the dark horses of this land, someone who knew what they entailed and didn't hesitate in using the utmost force in demonstrating the level of velocity they unmistakably had.

Samuel leaned in close to the young witch with a cheeky smile ensuring he hovered just below her left ear. "Ha, your tainted magical trickery doesn't work here! You're in my world now, girl!" Samuel grinned at her with a smolder. "Now let's go to my humble home and you can see just what you can be. Come on now. Don't be a peasant. I don't have much time for rebellious dawdling."

Samuel kept his sharp blue eyes on her just in case he'd have to reach over and drag her along with him. He was being formal although he was maintaining the comedic level. He kept the atmosphere between him and Isra as light as he possibly could, for darkness very much consumed her inside and out. And he had the slightest inkling that she might have tried to accost away from him at any given moment if he took his eyes off her just for a second.

Yet again with a snap of his thumb and index finger, Samuel and Isra were transported to his desired destination in a flash.

Isra twirled her head around only for her lime green eyes to fall upon acres of lush green pastures dotted with sweet violets and yellow crocuses. This was further dominated by a tall gray castle that stood out amongst the rest. It was almost as high as the clouds themselves. Of course, this was the majestic land of Spirisity. Only

Samuel or someone attuned to the realm themselves could materialize here. There was a sacred lock in which if you weren't accepted by the ones in the know, you wouldn't have a hope in hell of getting in. Excuse the pun, but that was the way it was engineered.

"So this is your domain?" Isra questioned Samuel with a wide-eyed glance.

It was as though she was shocked that the light bringer inhabited such a vast and vivid world filled with color and the slightest tinge of magic. Amazing when she considered the idea that apparently everything on the light side was dull and boring, but just looking upward at Samuel's majestic gray castle tower, she found herself quite entranced and intrigued by it.

"Yes. It's not much, but it does me well enough for my somewhat superior needs. I'm quite a boss in these parts. Some would say I'm a little demanding," Samuel joked whilst maintaining his friendly yet also smug smile. Again, he was being deliberate in keeping the atmosphere between him and Isra benevolent. "Anyhow, that's enough chatter for now, Missy. I must say I'm most intrigued to learn as to what the 'on high' has in store for me."

He chortled light-heartedly only to put his hand across his mouth in a haphazard manner. *Oh darn, I just mentioned the 'on high.' Goodness gracious, I hope she does not catch on to what I was referring to. She's a smart one, this girl. Although I realize she dumbs herself down to impress others. It is simply just an illusion.* Samuel mulled over this quietly in his thoughts.

Samuel often referred to the "on high" when he conversed with Astrid and James about the mission at hand. They were the sacred light bringers association. Almost like an organization that dealt with light versus dark and fought the intense battle that was always lingering in the background. They would be the folks you would communicate with when you needed some crucial insight that the mortal world simply could not deliver. The gracious beings at "on high" were being dead secretive of the ways and the rules of their world and kept everything very much hushed up unless you happened to be someone that they declared worthy of knowing.

It's true that Samuel was the chief light bringer, but even he was very much in the dark when it came to the wondrous beings at the "on high." It was a need-to-know basis even with him, but he was very much a hands-on type when it came to the fight against darkness. Samuel didn't mind getting his hands dirty if it meant that the light would win.

Samuel returned his attention to Isra with the intention to rectify his mistake immediately, only being too careful to give her eye contact, for the witch's wandering lime green eyes were practically ablaze with inquisitive puzzlement as she opened her mouth to say the words he dreaded.

"'On high?' Just what is that feisty conundrum?" Isra inquired, still giving Samuel a wide-eyed stare.

"You know, I think I may have made a slight faux pas in my wording. Please excuse my miscommunication. Now, shall we go in?" Samuel pardoned himself, hoping it was enough to disguise his ghastly blunder from Isra's avid curiosity.

"Wait..." Isra said.

Her eyes were all over the robust scenery that surrounded her. A quaint mass of greenery amongst sweet violets and yellow crocuses was not entirely how she had envisioned this transcendental land. Of course, she presumed it was a region that was distinctly cut off from the rest of the netherworld, somewhere that you could only get to if you were lucid dreaming, or perhaps it was simply just a realm that was untouchable unless you possessed the desired key to unlock it.

"You call yourself a light bringer, is that so? Well, th-this place..." Isra stammered unapologetically, trailing off as the realization of exactly where she was located dawned on her at once. "...is an expansion of time in another compass not known by many?"

She awaited Samuel's answer with great impatience. Having only imagined what it would be like to touch, see, and feel in an alternate reality was entrancing enough, but to be stood in a domain that was beyond her immortal comprehension that she could view with her own eyes and being completely conscious in the ethereal moment was a little bit too much for the witch to take.

"Erm, yes. It is." Samuel agreed although he seemed nervous that Isra was so thirsty for knowledge over his precious yet mysterious realm.

It was as though he wanted to drag her into his grand stature of a home and then she'd say nothing more about it. But of course, such an act would look suspicious. Samuel didn't want to appear as though he was engineering a cover up, but he'd rather just conceal the whole affair from her prying eyes.

"Anyhow, time is wasting with us being out here standing around and gawking. So let us go inside and we can have a more intimate chat about your predisposed predicament. Come now!" he ordered in a brash tone as he waved his index finger, indicating her to come forward to him.

There is much to be done, Samuel thought to himself with a sigh. *And I really need a stiff drink already! The day has only just really begun in theory and there is so much more that has yet to be thrown into my etheric field and God only knows how I will handle it!*

The light bringer mused to himself in quiet silence as Isra slowly made her way to him.

3

____

A trail of gray smoke billowed out from the chimney of a run-down, peach-colored hovel resembling a domicile where one could apparently live. It was a small yet compact building consisting of stone and all around were transparent glass panes that were barely held together by their iron framing.

The residency was sat on top of a singed yellow-mustard and fern-green grassy square that had clearly been burnt in a violent attack. Grass no longer grew in several places where the square had been cremated to a crisp in whatever occurrence had led to the affliction. Amongst the tiny home was a mass of open space of yellow and orange sheen; again, it had all been destroyed and weathered away as time had passed. Whatever this place had been before, it was just a wasteland now. The only question was who would be desperate enough to dwell in a bleak home such as this?

It was fortuitous because the answer reared its head inquisitively, peeking through the transparent glass window and looking out onto the scorched grassland that surrounded the derelict fortress. Everilda had been living in this wretched hovel for a few days, having found it unoccupied and left in such a horrendous state. And although the former witch was grateful for the shelter, she looked in dismay as she surveyed the poor condition of something that once upon a time must have been a very plentiful and richly decorated residence.

Inside wasn't much better. It was plain. Nothing but a simple yet dainty cottage where the walls were that of solemn gray brickwork. Of course, it was no surprise that the gray bricks of stone were slapped together haphazardly so you could see the cracks in between them. Whoever had dwelled in this forsaken place before had neglected to fill in the crevices with a generous helping of cement so that the cold could be kept out. Despite the dreary gray stone bricks and lack of finery here, there was a rather endowed black ebony fireplace gracing the back wall so at least there was some warmth in the room. Coals cauterized making loud hissing noises as they became incinerated at the bottom of the fire pit.

Everilda extended her hands over to the fire, holding them out in mid air above the hot, searing coals in the attempt to warm her cold and bony fingers. Her hands were in quite disarray. You could see several patches across the tops of her hands where parts of her skin had peeled away from the sheer dry conditions they had been exposed to. Everilda had adorned her precious hands in black fingerless gloves but the leather was so worn and tattered that they barely kept the icy chill out.

It went without notice that Everilda was annoyed she had allowed herself to live in this disgraceful manner, but she'd hardly had a choice in the matter. Resentment hammered through her soul as she imagined coming into contact with Isra, just for a moment or two to lay into the witch she'd once called friend and putting out all her anger and pent-up frustration onto Isra. Revenge was sorely on the forefront of Everilda's mind.

It didn't matter as far as Everilda was concerned that she had tried in vain to get Isra banished from the Wingdom's Academy by callously lying to old Magnus about her. She had felt her actions were indeed justified, that she had more or less paved the way for a severe reprimand headed directly in Isra's domain by telling a tall tale to the pompous old wombat that was Mr. Wingdom's himself.

Everilda had felt as if she was doing Wingdom's a favor if nothing else by spouting out a load of nonsense about Isra. She had felt it was a disservice to her personally by Wingdom's stripping her of her powers. After all, witches were in Everilda's blood. Her father had been a most profound and also greatly feared warlock during his tenure where he'd done the most frowned upon acts in order to succumb to his own immortal greed.

~

DAMIEN DAUGHTRY WAS a young man barely any older than sixteen when he first entered Wingdom's welcoming doors, but he'd been trouble from the start.

Damien had unleashed havoc into the supposedly peaceful school for young witches and warlocks alike when he'd summoned the demonic entity Rhiannon who had surged upon the once unisex training academy like a hellish plague. She first put a hex upon the female population in the academy so that they engaged in sexual acts and thus became impure. Next Rhiannon, who was not satisfied with her handiwork, placed a curse upon Wingdom's so that every female soul that entered into the stately establishment would be doomed to become tempted unto the darkness. She felt this was justice personified as she had been plunged into Hell many years before, which made her the demonic self she was.

It was no surprise to everyone when Magnus Wingdom banished and exiled all males from the academy after that in order to prevent any further impure incidents. However, not many that entered into the premises thereafter had ever known its unisex history unless they were brash enough to delve into the archives of Wingdom's history; such information would remain a mystery.

Damien was a headstrong one though and he had fallen for Rhiannon despite her baneful personality. She was sultry in her long black attire of a dress that clung to every inch of her voluptuous hourglass figure, dangling her long shiny burgundy red hair that tipped down just below her shoulders. The vengeful demon had lured the modest yet handsome Damien into her claws and they'd consummated their lust when he gave into the wicked, willful temptations she had thrust his way.

However, later it was announced that Damien was to enter into an arranged marriage with a mortal noblewoman, as his mother Marie wanted to steer her son as far away from damnation as best she could. And so, Damien painfully bid Rhiannon goodbye, but she never quite let go, for it was later revealed that when Damien wed his betrothed sweetheart Damaris, Rhiannon wasn't going to allow him to be free.

The cold-hearted and harsh-willed demoness had found out all about Damien's impending nuptials and had stormed the ceremony, promising revenge if he'd had the sheer nerve to go through with it. Rhiannon shrieked at Damien, beseeching him and his newlywed wife Damaris. She delivered her fatal curse: "I decree that from this day and every day that follows, you shall both be cursed."

There was a short pause as the terrified Damaris hid behind her newly married husband as Rhiannon enacted her promise with pungent malice and violent fiery flame. Green and black flames encompassed Rhiannon as she spoke. "But when you give birth to your first-born child Damaris, she will not only be a product of dark-hearted fervor and callous destruction, but as my earthly daughter she will belong to *me*. When the young girl finds that darkness reigns upon her heart, then and only then will I reveal her true heritage. For she is mine!" And with that, Rhiannon departed, never, ever to be seen again.

One year passed and all seemed peaceful between Damaris and Damien, but it was then that Damaris gave birth to her daughter, Everilda. It appeared as though both Damien and Damaris had forgotten about Rhiannon's deadly curse, for they seemed blissfully happy; however, Damien was still a purebred warlock at heart. It was also in his blood. Having found he was unable to tear himself away from his destructive personality, he finally left Damaris a year after Everilda's birth, as he was to pursue being one of the world's most loathsome yet handsome foes.

Damien found summoning deadly entities far more entertaining than raising a family. It was likely that Rhiannon played a part in

Damien's fearsome career in being villainous and wicked. But it was after Everilda turned one-year-old that all news of Damien and Rhiannon dried up. And so nobody was aware that either fierce malevolence was even in existence anymore.

IT GOES without saying that Everilda had no clue of her immortal heritage except that her father Damien was a warlock who had deserted her gypsy mother Damaris without warning one day. And after that, just like the rest of the world, Everilda knew very little about what had become of Damien Daughtry.

The blonde-haired wannabe-villainess tore herself away from the fire, having felt that it provided no warmth and was only fueling the envious fire inside her heart. She had not seen nor talked to Isra since Magnus banished her and thus removed her unsightly powers from her person, but the fair-haired Everilda was curious as to what might commence if she and Isra happened to be in close proximity to each other.

Just what fun could Everilda have if she happened to goad Isra into doing something absolutely terrible? Something horrifically unjust that could cause Isra to be seen for what Everilda believed she was: the villain of the piece, blood thirsty and seeking vengeance just like Everilda was at this precise moment.

"And what might the thunderous folk at Wingdom's do then? Perhaps they'd deal with Isra in a similar manner as they did so with me. Maybe then she'd be rendered powerless and mortal and I'd finally get the upper hand. Maybe my glory could be well and truly restored in their eyes," Everilda said evilly with a smirk.

4

Samuel watched Isra closely as he poured her a strong mug of black coffee almost as dark as the atmosphere between them. Isra had been sitting there in his humble abode for about an hour now and she had shown no signs of changing her mind in relation to her dark path. Neither did she seem awfully interested in anything Samuel had to say regarding the lighter way of life, but by golly was he going to try to make Isra see that the grass really was greener on the other side, literally, for Spirisity was covered in fine green pastures.

But Samuel was determined even more so to get Isra to see things from his perspective, to have her on his wavelength in the way he saw the world, to swing Isra into Samuel's broad-minded way of thinking and show her that there was more to life than just being out there unleashing absolute chaos unto the cosmos.

"Do you take sugar? I am not quite sure." Samuel paused with a half-smile while also taking a very stiff and yet serious glance. "To be honest with you, dear girl, I don't know that much about you. Do tell me how all this came to pass!" He insisted on an answer, leaving the bowl of sugar on the same cream-colored China saucer that he'd placed the cup of coffee on.

"It's a long story," Isra mouthed.

She hesitated in looking Samuel in the eye as she wrapped her hands around the hot mug of black coffee, looking down into its somber contents swirling in the cup. She took a small sip but concentrated on keeping her gaze cast down at the floor, just in case Samuel was metaphysically sensing anything about her.

You know, in a supernatural way, how you could just look into somebody's eyes and see everything there is to know about them? All the good and the really grotesque, nitty-gritty stuff that you wouldn't dare to expose unless there was something you could get out of it.

"I have time to hear it. I bet it's nothing that I haven't heard a hundred times before. Indulge my whimsical interest," Samuel insisted as he placed his cup of coffee back down upon the saucer, now giving Isra his undivided attention, for he wanted to ensure that she felt she was being listened to because now was a crucial time in the young witch's life.

"I am not sure it is terribly noteworthy for an assured man such as yourself," Isra replied with a sharp, broody glance.

Clearly eyeing the light bringer up, her piercing lime green eyes flashed all over him, almost burning into him as she didn't take her focus away, not for one moment which should have made even the most inscrutable beings nervous. But Samuel didn't even flinch. Instead, he allowed Isra to do her visual soul seeking and whatever it was she felt she needed to do to prove that he was indeed trustworthy.

Well, she's been betrayed more times than she cares to count, who can blame her for wanting to test if I am the legitimate item? Samuel perused in his thoughts. *I can only imagine the heartache she's been through time and time again and so it's only natural for her to suspect that I am going to do the exact same thing. She trusts no one. I get that. But somehow, we need to change her thinking on the ways and means of people. She needs to see that not every person in her life is going to behave in that manner. And that not everybody will be as treacherous as the ones she has known.*

Samuel paused again as he took another long, drawn-out sip of his coffee, musing over the idea that Isra could tell her tale however she saw it, but all he could do was listen and be on hand to offer advice if she deemed him worthy enough to do so.

"I am sure it is for the right soul to hear. How do you know if you don't try, hmm?" he pressed gently. "Come on; make my day slightly more bearable than it has been all morning. I bet it is riveting." Samuel added a slight half smile, subtly winking at Isra as his bold, blue eyes met smack-bang in the middle with Isra's own.

"Well, it all started out with just me and Everilda. Everi, I called her for short. I had only just come here and she was new as well, so we met at the same stage of training at Wingdom's Academy. Therefore, we both had that as common ground," Isra explained, looking at Samuel as she recalled meeting Everilda for the first time.

Her glimmering green eyes were almost lit up with warm enthusiasm for the story as they burned brighter for the first time she had gone dark. Luminescent neon green flared in them like flaming embers upon an open fire.

Goes with the feeling that our witch is indeed a little firecracker, Samuel commented to himself in quiet thought. Samuel saw that Isra had neglected to continue and so he waved his hand at her in an inviting manner as he said, "Everilda. Yes. Go on girl!"

Isra almost gushed for a second. Her face was ever so close to making a rare smile appear on it before she too made a hand gesture, but hers was defensive in nature as she folded her arms, pressing them in a bold stance over her chest. It was a protective measure as well for those who were selective in their conversation for fear they would be hurt or even betrayed. It was a very common act for those who guarded themselves, such as Isra.

"And then one day, Everilda was out. I was supposed to meet her, but surprise, she never turned up. Anyway, that was when I met Jonathan. My beau. Or at least he was supposed to be," Isra muttered with a furrowed brow.

The once glimmering light in her eyes had completely vanished now and nothing but dark holes remained. The light had been obliterated. It was obvious Isra talking about Jonathan was painful and it also made Isra very angry, as though she could implode at any moment, but for some reason she was calm, situated in her black leather cushioned seat with her back pressed against it so hard that Samuel was sure if she forced it anymore, she'd rupture her spine in two.

"Oh." Samuel motioned again before waving his hand again to signal her to carry on.

He was enjoying her bemusing and yet also intriguing tale, but he already knew some of it. Of course, he did; he'd known about Isra for long enough. He just didn't know all of the details firsthand. He wasn't Astrid. Samuel hadn't swooped down and carefully pinned his eyes on his chosen prey as he kept watch on her every single step. But of course, that had also been engineered by Samuel ... well, at least some of it, anyhow.

Isra wasn't exactly forthcoming with the enlightening information that Samuel deeply desired to have attained, so he prodded with a little gentle nudging as he gave her a charismatic smile while being formal in his mannerisms. His arms were slightly pressed together before they came apart in an emotionally quiet stance.

"And this young man turned out not to be the charming man you had envisioned him as? Perhaps he disappointed your predisposed illusions of what you had aspired to happen in the romantic aspect of things," Samuel presumed while also suggesting something that would be both thought-provoking and triggering to Isra.

Yes, he had deliberately suggested that she had illusions in relation to love. Maybe Isra was more in love with the idea of it than the person she had imagined herself with. Samuel knew better than anyone that in order for one to heal first, the oppressed emotion must be brought up to the surface. And then they could either accept it or be so deep in fear they'd reject it, leaving themselves in the exact state they were before the trigger was released and thus nothing would change. No healing would ever commence. And with Isra, this was a likely outcome.

"Something like that. Yes, he wasn't what I had hoped. It's no secret that I was disappointed beyond measure," Isra explained. Her voice grew more coarse as if this expression of the turmoil she had experienced with the hapless Jonathan had indeed triggered her.

Samuel could only smile back at her, for he was triumphant in knowing his plan had worked. He had got her talking finally, and perhaps now he could impart his own advice on how he thought she could take charge of things from here on out. And no. That didn't mean summoning more dragons or anything else that those "on high" would strictly frown upon.

Samuel twiddled his thumb and forefinger together for a second, clearly very anxious at what he was about to propose to the witch. He was nervous, that was true. It was unusual for Samuel to act this way, but even he, the most powerful light bringer in the land, the righteous and worldly man that was at the top of his game, yes, even he had fears. But in every serious conundrum of course there is a glimmer of hope waiting in the wings for one to grasp onto.

And he had a right to be worried about how he would be received because Samuel was about to turn up the heat in his interrogation. He wasn't playing around here. This wasn't some game! He was doing his utmost to dig into what made Isra the way she was at heart because ultimately, he wanted to fix her in a sense. It was odd that Samuel was becoming attached to a subject of his that he was supposed to "deal" with, but there was just something so vulnerable about Isra that he couldn't help but find an endearment toward her. Oh yes, she was goofy in places despite her rough stone-cold demeanor that she demonstrated to the universe, but Samuel knew that was just a very well-orchestrated act.

"Incredible, and how did it turn sour, if you don't mind my asking??" Samuel inquired, forcing his back further against his red velvet chair.

He'd forgotten how much he adored that chair. He was so relaxed that a stray strand of his black slicked back hair collapsed from his normally precise mane. Samuel was subtle in excusing the mishap as he fiddled with his unruly fringe, setting the pesky loose hair back into place before he combed his jet-black smooth hair back. He gave himself a look in the mirror that was affixed to the wall just beside his grand throne of a chair before returning his attention to Isra.

"Ah yes, sorry about that. My sincere apologies. It does get a little mischievous at times." Samuel motioned as he relaxed back against his chair, folding his hands together in a prayer stance. "Please carry on."

Isra resisted the urge to giggle at Samuel's queer fascination with fixing his hair but as she caught herself staring into the light bringer's eyes, she noticed just how bright the blue truly was. It was almost the color of sapphire. An entire ocean could be found in those mesmerizing eyes of his. Soft yet bold hues of rich azure mixed with the soft sheen of the sky. It was like something from another cosmos inside those round globes of mystery. However, Isra had forgotten she was in another macrocosm beyond anyone's imagination at this precise moment in time.

She continued, although there was a small pause between her and Samuel where she pondered over whether she should divulge this part of the story.

There was something wonderfully attractive and charismatic about this man. And it was true that Samuel wasn't the type of man she would normally choose out of millions; however, she did find him magnetizing to say the least. It would be fair to say that Samuel appeared very alluring and at the same time quite mysterious to the very young Isra.

"It was fine at first. I didn't notice any signs that something was amiss, but later Everilda was strange with me. She was very bitter and callous in the way she spoke about my courting this man she had no knowledge of. But then it emerged she had known way more than she had claimed to, as I caught her and Jonathan having a blazing row outside my coven. So, in the end, my best friend betrayed me."

Isra finished abruptly. She tapped her fingers anxiously on Samuel's desk and he noted her rough yet smooth manner in which she was acting cool when really she was resisting the urge to blow in an almighty way.

"Things between me and Everilda have not been the same since," Isra hastened to add at the end.

And that was it. She had let the final puzzle piece fall into place for Samuel who now had every fragment of the story of what had commenced just before Isra went dark. Samuel smiled, pausing for a second as his hands came together once again in a prayer stance, but this time he had an expression up his face as though he had just found gold. A subtle yet happy moment in which the light bringer in a very rare juncture emitted joy.

He turned to Isra with a furrowed brow. He was wide eyed as he stared at her with ambiguity. He was unsure of how receptive she would be to what he had to offer, but surely it had to be better than the current ensemble of a life she was living? Don't assume for one moment Samuel was unsympathetic toward Isra's plight and her reasoning for switching sides, but he knew better than anyone that a life touched by darkness was not particularly abundant. And eventually it would catch the attention of those who suffered similarly because those energies flocked to one another like maggots on a rotting corpse.

Samuel motioned forward, giving Isra a much more concerning look as he muttered, "You know there is a better way than all this..." He seemed to hesitate as he tried to fathom the right word to describe the things she was enacting, "...unnecessary *pain!*"

Samuel blurted out the last of his words, slowly withdrawing from her and sliding back into his chair so he was slightly further away from her position. He had hoped he had picked the right word and not one that would trigger her.

"What do you mean?" Isra piped up with curiosity. For a second there her eyes lit up a more radiant shade of jade green. So, the light bringer had firmly accosted her attention.

"I mean, you could be doing something fulfilling with your life instead of this..." Again, Samuel struggled to find the words he needed. A perplexed grin suggested he was seeking one that was both empathetic and tactful. "This darkness and mayhem." He hoped he wasn't sounding contradictory. The last thing he needed was Isra thinking he was some kind of narrow minded, pompous imbecile.

"Mayhem?" she questioned in an eager voice as though she half believed that what Samuel was trying to impart to her was true.

Samuel waved his fingers awkwardly before allowing them to float on the tabletop in midair, gently tapping the table as he laid out his proposition, slowly muttering the words one by one in a formal yet also endearing way.

"There could be something more..." he drawled out in a low voice.

Samuel had also softened his tone quite dramatically as though he may have been talking to a child. He was very careful with his hand gestures and also more importantly his words because any kind of meaning could be misinterpreted. Who knows what kind of bloodshed could follow if Isra got the wrong end of the stick?

"More than the preempted violence that is masquerading as a warped, undefined power trip."

Samuel tried to explain although perhaps he wasn't being quite as sensitive as he had in mind, as Isra flared up immediately. The porcelain, fine-boned, peach cheeks turned bright, beetroot red and honestly, and it was hard to decipher whether she was insulted or angry. There was also the slight tinge of defensiveness that could be detected as she voiced her disapproval.

"I don't see it as warped," Isra countered. Her voice was almost high pitched like she wanted to scream but yet somehow, she was maintaining a civil composure.

Let's face it; she could probably shoot lightning bolts out of her eye sockets if she really wanted to. So the fact she was calm for the moment was bemusing to say the least. Samuel must be doing something right if she was managing to stay so well contained within her "lighter" exterior.

"Well, maybe you should look at it from the light bringer point of view."

He continued to urge her cautiously as he was trying to be diplomatic. Samuel was trying to convey his point of view although it was baffling for her to comprehend why she should change things around, as it would only be a matter of time before someone got wind of her transmutation and then things could really get dire for her. Being dark was one thing, but it was another entity entirely to be shown a pathway to escape that said imprisonment and not take them up on it. The light bringer community "on high" tended to regard such matters very seriously and would deal with them in any way they saw fit.

"People, well, those who have abilities like yourself but have chosen to use them in a more enriching way," Samuel began quietly while rubbing his hands together as if he was preparing for something as he breathed nervously into his hands.

"You mean the goody-two-shoes types? The person that walks among unicorns and rainbows and delights in the beauty of this wonderful glowing cosmos?"

Isra chided Samuel in a sarcastic and also annoying tone, as if she found the whole idea rather repulsive, like it wasn't really satisfying enough for her being. That living in the mundane world showered with sun rays of light and with little bells attached to her feet as if she was some magnificently soft docile creature that never dared to be anything else.

"I think the term or phrase you are looking for is *enlightened*," Samuel reprimanded her softly, almost getting ready to pounce down and give her a good old verbal ear bashing. For the witch although young and burdened by her set of circumstances was beginning to border past insolence as far as he was concerned.

"Yes, but many would refer to it as dull and boring," Isra reminded him with a harsher glare than the previous one.

Yes, she had been insulted and now she was showing him her full wrath. Those emerald green eyes of hers appeared to resemble cherries as bright red brashness dominated her pupils which only highlighted her irritation.

"You see it as boring and that is the problem here. The thing is, you could turn this around. It wouldn't have to be as you perceive it. Excitement can be found in the most unmeasured of places if only one dared to try it on for size," Samuel recited as though he was reading something out of a rule book.

However, what he was trying his utmost to emphasize was that it might not be what Isra believed it to look like. For she had never ever done it so how could she possibly know what that kind of path would look like for her? Had she seen the glimmering green apples dangling from the tree stained with their luscious ruby red that the normal paved road didn't seem as entrancing to her now? Or was there more to this that Samuel wasn't quite grasping?

Perhaps fear lurked closer to home in Isra's heart than he had presumed; however, he was getting somewhere with her. Much further than anyone in her life had ever got so there was progress being made although it may have seemed small. It was quite possible that Samuel was rubbing off on Isra in a very positive way. The young blonde-haired witch looked at Samuel as if he was a creature from another land. Something that was either so predestined or so far removed from human society that nobody could understand what they were really about.

Samuel's strange, unorthodox ways of communicating through a difficult situation must have seemed so otherworldly to Isra especially when she was used to people walking away when she did something they disagreed with. It must have been a real soul shocker to find someone that was actually interested in getting to the root of the problem. And Samuel was really invested in doing just that but not just that.

No, he was interested in getting to know Isra, personally in the sense that he might be her therapist and her best friend rolled into one, with the hope that both entities would congregate well enough with each other to come to a positive resolution or at least one that didn't end in sheer damnation.

"It's not really something I am desperately seeking at this time. I mean, I am sure sooner or later it may come across as appealing if I stumble across a whim of tiresome boredom, but until such time I think I shall refrain," Isra commented with a sneer.

Now it was apparent that she was becoming annoyed. She was

becoming more stiff as the minutes went on, slouching impatiently in that leather hard backed chair that James normally sat in while also fiddling with her long golden tresses. Yes, she was getting rather irked with this conversation but at least she had heard Samuel out. That was something that could be said for her.

"Well, if that is your wish, I can do nothing to counteract it. But remember that while you are in the dark world, you will be watched very closely by my wandering and watchful eye." Samuel raised a warning finger at her as he spoke. "However, be that as it may, you have listened to my words and I appreciate your time, Isra. I will send you back now exactly as you were and you will be no worse off for having this little intimate chat with me."

Samuel motioned to her with a wide-eyed grin, but he stopped short of finishing his sentence, leaving a long silence lingering between him and Isra.

"But I must warn you, girl. You are on our radar now. If we catch you doing anything that may come across as close to grotesque, you will be dealt with, understand?"

Samuel spoke to her in a brassy tone. It was as though he meant business because he wasn't going to play around when it came to matters of the dark side. Isra opened her mouth in the guise she was about to say something in denial or refusal to cooperate with the warning he had given her, but Samuel stopped her before she could even muster such a pitiful excuse not to abide by it.

"Oh, and that wasn't a question." Samuel finished, waving his index finger yet again signaling he wasn't messing about. His face was enough to indicate he was serious and was not about to be tried with.

"All right then, if that is all..." Isra concurred, proceeding to lift her hand to wave herself away, but again she was interrupted by Samuel who could only glance at her with an amused stare although he was still being quite stuffy with her.

"You'd do well to remember that your magic will not work in my realm! Any material created from darkness does not get to live within the walls of Spirisity. So don't attempt to make another move." He cajoled her with a wide-eyed grin before remembering that he'd be sending her back and that perhaps it was a good idea to let her know this so she wouldn't look at him so confused. "I'll be using my magical ways and means to send you back to your land. And don't worry, you'll find yourself at the mountain crevice in a flash!" he uttered softly.

Isra piped up at this announcement as she suddenly found that she'd rather be elsewhere. There was unfinished business and somewhere that she really needed to get back to and if possible in a hurry. "Do you mind if you pop me back to Wingdom's Academy rather than that mountain peak? It's just I..." she trailed off, not finishing what she was about to mention, for she realized that might indeed draw the attention where she didn't want it to go.

Damn, he probably already knows. He may as well be reading me right at this moment. Oh hell, beseech me because I yearn for revenge against my foes. I'll likely be smacked down for that longing too! Isra murmured to herself in thought. She considered the idea of eavesdropping on the situation with Everilda since she had not heard anything for a while as she put her tenure at Wingdom's behind her. There was just the need to inform them of her wholly decision.

Samuel paid no attention to Isra's vile mind chatter; he could clearly gather she had plans to squander off someplace else from here so he simply winked at her, only taking in the fact that this was a more serious matter than he had thought.

"Very well." Samuel acknowledged her in a lower voice before lifting his right hand into the air, preparing to send her on her merry way. It was with a wave of his hand that the esteemed Isra appeared still annoyed at Samuel as white light hues gathered their forces around her. Then she began to dematerialize in the space of a nano second while a white fluffy cloud-like energy made her seem as though she was fading away.

Samuel smiled once more as she departed, although a faint whiff of strawberry was noted by Samuel's extraordinary paranormal senses. It was so pungent he could almost salivate over it even though there was nothing physical there.

"Interesting. Such a nice flavor for a girl of her age," he noted out loud although nobody was around to hear his comment, thankfully.

Samuel looked over to the spot where Isra had been sitting. She had long left him finally, but after such an awkward and also very insightful conversation, Samuel now knew that things were much more knee-deep than he had originally estimated. It was time to strike down hard and fast. If they were going to win this mission against Isra darkness, it was time they did something about it. And there was no time to lose.

"It is time to send in the novel and esoteric James."

He will put a spanner or two in her way, Samuel thought to himself with glee, resisting the urge to burst out into involuntary laughter because the way he had things planned, James was about to turn Isra's world upside down and she'd never see it coming.

5

Samuel took in the scent of his strong caffeinated beverage for a second before turning to the onlooker seated before him. Although he had a forewarning glower upon his face, there was also a tangible hint of amusement for what he was about to do pertaining to the lady in question. Miss Isra.

"Thank you for coming at such short notice," Samuel greeted as he poured his guest an equally steaming mug of hot, bitter coffee. There was honestly no better beverage for such an intimate and important discussion.

"It's not an inconvenient timing although I did have other plans," a low rumbling male voice erupted with a marginally huffy tone as though there was somewhere else they'd rather be. Or perhaps he was just wholly pissed off over something, but he graciously accepted the welcoming cup of caffeine that Samuel handed his way. The fact that he was quite exhausted already made him indebted.

Samuel continued to enunciate his exact plans as he threw himself back into his elegant red velvet chair, evidently taking his role as light bringer to its fullest as he motioned toward his guest with a no-nonsense fleeting look.

"I appreciate I have disturbed you from whatever is hitting the surface right now James, but there are greater matters at hand. As an agent of the 'on high,' I shouldn't have to refresh your memory of what your responsibilities are," Samuel responded with a warm glance. "But it is of much deeper magnitude than we had thought," he added as he met an amazingly confused glance from James who had no idea of what unearthing Samuel was about to lie at his domain.

"How so?" James inquired, pursing his lips and then hastily taking a sip of his coffee before exhaling a long drawn-out breath that was so everlasting it may have provoked the question as to whether or not he was anxious over something.

"I have met with our witch in question," Samuel retold James in a cautionary tone although his disposition was very much relaxed. "And as nice as she is, I would say she is very much about to dabble into much deeper realms than I had anticipated." Samuel stopped to take a quaff of his bitter drink which had now gone cold much to Samuel's resentment. He really did detest cold coffee. It was definitely on his list of pet peeves.

"Oh," James retorted sharply. It seemed he was not surprised by this remark as there was literally no reaction from him.

"I have seen that she has so far summoned a dragon, and despite having quite the intimate chat with our vengeful foe, she has no desire to change it around. I would describe her as rebellious, strong willed, and very determined to do exactly as she sees fit. This means she is not only darkening her own heart but others are at risk too, for any life that becomes attached to her is also at risk of sheer damnation," Samuel explained with a look of concern as now he was viewing this as a very urgent matter that needed a lot of due care and attention.

"Hmm. I have witnessed similar in my contact with her as well as Astrid..." James trailed off.

It was much to the bemusement of Samuel who had no inkling whatsoever that James had encountered Isra and was completely baffled as to how this event had come to pass without his knowing of it.

"What do you mean, in *your* contact with her? I was led to believe you had not met her as of yet?" Samuel pressed James.

Samuel gave James the impression that he was about to pound his heavy, pent-up, anger-filled fists upon his desk in frustration of something else coming apart that he knew nothing about.

Nobody says a damn thing to me about the whole shebang and they wonder why I get righteously pissed at them! Goodness, save my sanity, for I feel I am about to lose my mind. These blasted peasants and their lack of communiqué, Samuel ranted reverently to himself.

If it wasn't just Astrid doing it, he was bound to assume that others were doing so as well.

"I have spoken to Astrid once about his lack of finesse when it comes to Isra and she just so happened to be in the vicinity at the time. So I froze the scene. She didn't even know I was there," James recalled with valiant enthusiasm as he remembered giving Astrid a good old-fashioned reprimand for yet again being in places he shouldn't have.

Samuel drawled out a long sigh of relief. Finally, it seemed like he was pleased about something in this mass struggle of conflicting events that all seemed to bind together and calibrate as one.

"Oh, so you two didn't actually have a physical meeting then? Right, I see. Big confusion here. Sorry; long day." Samuel enunciated carefully, feeling like he should be chugging down enormous gulps of heavy whiskey instead of his favorite caffeinated beverage.

"It's no quandary, really. I get it," James stated.

It didn't take a genius to come to the conclusion that the immense pressure Samuel was under with this mission was getting to him quite a bit. Being the guy who made the tough decisions was one thing, but berating those around him for not doing what he deemed right, making him seem like the baddie was a lot harder. Samuel didn't want any misconceptions made over his character, but sometimes he was the one who had to do the things nobody else could. The choices that others couldn't bear to make. The decisions that nobody else had the guts to decide. Samuel was the guy who had to do it and, in the end, and that made his job just that little bit more challenging.

"Right, well, back to the matter at hand. There's a tower, a sort of citadel that has been empty for eons now. I want to slot our Isra into there. But it must look like an accident, you see? We can't have her delving into the pitted veins of her dark, saturated brain and piecing all this together. It needs to look like a common occurrence. Well, I guess we should get started then. Oh, and let's not speak about this with Astrid. If he gets wind of it, we may have some unwanted interference. We cannot have that, James!" Samuel emphasized with a furrowed brow although his smile resembled some kind of hidden agenda.

"I understand," James concurred earnestly.

"Good, then we have no more to discuss. Remember. Discretion in all forms," Samuel said in a low voice.

But little did those two fine men know that someone had not only overheard their delightful conversation that they had thought to be secret, but that same someone was now furious as he fought to keep his footing on the window ledge.

Astrid the raven kept his fury and anger in as he slid away from the corner of the window ledge, having been perched there throughout the entire duration of the conversation, and now he was absolutely seething.

Best move fast before they realize I'm here, Astrid thought to himself as he arched his black, silky wings in preparation to disappear into the light. *And I can't stay now that I know what I know. I'm so beyond pissed. How dare they do this without my knowledge? You'd think that they'd at least include me since I've been in on it since day one!* Astrid ranted away sullenly, cursing both Samuel and James in thought as he was almost ready to take off.

"So they think they can do all this and I won't have a clue, huh? They think they can shut me out and pretend I've never been involved? Wow, I never knew they could be so callous. They don't want me to know, hmmm? Okay, I'll play their silly little human games. They think I don't know. Oh yes, but the trouble is I know way more than I claim to. Eventually a time will come when they discover just how much I'm aware of that I'm not supposed to," Astrid chuckled to himself as he brought himself forward in flight. "I'll show those pitiful, insolent humans just exactly what I'm made of. Soon."

Astrid cawed as he coursed the skies, just about able to see since night was covering everything in sight. That cobalt blue almost black carpet painted the night sky, leaving only enough room for the bright tingling stars. And the raven knew exactly where he was going. The very same place that he was forbidden to be. Right in the midst of a certain lady.

Yet again, Astrid refused to obey orders. And did he care who knew what he was up to? Not really. Because now he was going to show the world just what he was really capable of.

6

———————

Rain pelted the land hard as if it was fighting back against an avalanche. The sky hurled it down onto the grass like fireballs of water. Although it was daylight, you could barely recognize the time of day since the sun was dormant, hiding away under the cover of cloud burst.

James approached his destination after a long, brisk walk from Spirisity, having decided that he couldn't just make himself appear here in a puff of smoke. If he was going to get this undercover lark exactly right, he'd have to act like he lived here in a normal, mundane manner. Acting and behaving like a human would in the physical realm meant walking as a means to get from one desired location to another.

Just up ahead stood the majestic realm that was Shambre Fell, the exact domain that Samuel spoke about at length. But hang on a second...

There was a brief pause. James was having a great deal of immeasurable hardship in trying to placate some of that discussion for the retentiveness of it seemed to be off. James shrugged it off as he glanced over at the sublime spectacle that stood before him. It was bigger than Samuel had described. Somehow James felt like

Samuel might have been underestimating its magnificence. That grayish-white tower alone shooting straight up into the sky almost was enough to make it stand out. It was just like a castle in some sense, but there was the tower and then a bit underneath. Of course, all of it was lined with the finest of jet-black iron window frames with the most crystal clear transparent glass in every single one.

There was more to this place than just that lonesome tower though. The greenery that surrounded Shambre Fell put the garden of Spirisity to shame. Acres of the most luscious green grass dominated the large square between the spiked tower, and there was of course the aqua blue stream that ran around Shambre Fell. An assortment of exquisite fruit trees ranging from cherry to plum were all delightfully ripe. Mouth-watering fruits hung off them like tempting treats just waiting to lure an innocent victim in. The most interesting part of the garden was the rose bushes that grew around the citadel itself. They were mostly red in coloring like a ruby, but as James observed, there were an odd few in shades of magenta and violet.

I guess this place has to be entrancing and enchanting otherwise nobody would want to live here. But I can't help but wonder if this is "on high's" handiwork as it seems so fake, James murmured to himself in thought.

"How the hell am I going to convince her that she needs to live here? Does she even have knowledge of it? I mean, how does one presume that she's going to even come across this fortress?" James questioned out loud for just about anyone to hear.

He imagined that Samuel was standing right next to him with that all-knowing, blunt answer that was something like, "Don't try and fathom the whys and wherefores of how it works; just allow it to be because you know there is a greater force at hand here." And James would be right to assume that would be the kind of comeback Samuel would deliver.

Of course, because in the scheme of things there is always something intangible that the naked eye cannot see but it's all laid out in preparation for the big finish. How stupid of me to lose sight of that for a second, James joked to himself in thought.

"All right then, so how does she fit into it? I mean, is she just going to materialize out of nowhere, or..." James trailed off, as suddenly a tall figure with fair hair in a midnight blue velvet cloak emerged out of nowhere. "What the hell?" James cursed under his breath in amazement of the female approaching him.

Long blonde, almost golden ringlets of hair stuck out of that velvety cloak. The only clear identifier was those piercing green eyes of hers. Yes, it was definitely Isra. But James was now wondering where on earth she had come from? There wasn't much time for a line of inquiry as the fair-haired witch was almost within eyes distance of James now. Her hair trailed behind her in the low winds as she emerged from the clearing amongst the trees.

"Hello, there. I am sorry to disturb your preoccupation," Isra muttered apologetically directly at James. "But I was told there was a humble abode around here somewhere that was vacant."

Isra immediately made James stop in his tracks, now questioning just how the witch knew. *Yes, and how did she know that? Has Samuel set this up so elaborately that he's told her in some form or another that is the place for her?* James thought to himself with a smug smirk.

Now he was starting to see the amusement in the situation. Really when he stopped and thought about it, Samuel's antics were pretty damn entertaining. This was a masterpiece of a plan and it was only just unfolding.

Wait, James suddenly probed himself for a second. *Did I just somehow summon her by imagining her being right next to me? This couldn't be, could it? I mean, it's not impossible but maybe I did indeed manifest her apparition before my very eyes,* James mused to himself in quiet solitude. *Stranger things have happened. And let's face it; I do have powers, although I am not sure if I am allowed to divulge exactly what I have the means to do. I am not quite sure if it would displease Samuel to have that information thrown about willy nilly. He may fear that it could get back to the wrong participant. So, what do I say to her, more to the point?*

She's clearly here for a reason and here I am considering what in damnation to say to her. It has to be Samuel. That sly old dog. He's behind all of this. Yes, that has to be it, James concurred, still in deliberation with himself.

Isra, although still waiting for James to answer her, stared out at the spindling tower ahead of her, realizing that this magnificent gray spike that shot up almost reaching out to the stars must be the legendary fortress she had been seeking.

"Oh, that must be it, yes?" Isra exclaimed.

It was a question, but her manner of speaking was her guessing that this must be the notorious Shambre Fell, but where she'd got that idea from James could only begin to imagine.

"Err, I am not sure. Wait, you mean this grand stature of a stronghold? I guess so," James answered. He was quick with it. He'd never had to think so fast in his life, honestly. He didn't expect to be in the presence of Isra so soon, so this was a bit of a shock to his system.

"Yes. I was told it is available for someone to dwell within its walls. I am looking for a base. Somewhere to spend my days and hide away from the not so favorable folk of this world," Isra answered with a fervent flavor.

"Ah. I see. So you need that kind of dwelling?" James probed her quizzically. "Oh, yes. I am James, by the way," he added almost stuttering the words, still shocked that she was here.

"Isra," she muttered in a formal manner.

"What brings you to Shambre Fell then? It's not really a location that many know about," James earnestly told her.

He wanted to get to the truth of why she was here of all places and seek the proof that he already knew deep inside himself, that Samuel had indeed orchestrated this whole thing and he'd gone as far to putting Isra in a place where she could likely do the least harm. Yes, because placing a witch inside a sheltered fortress away from prying eyes was certainly a most cunning plan indeed. Definitely the work of Samuel.

"I have unfortunately come to a phase in my life in which I have moved on from certain things. The time has come for me to move onto pastures new."

Isra spoke carefully, as she noticed that James was staring at her in a very standoffish way. It was as though maybe he didn't believe her story to be quite as true as she claimed. He unnerved her a little as he eyed her closely, focusing on those piercing green lime eyes of hers before examining her body language which was fixed in nature almost a little too precise for his liking. But there was something about the way she spoke. It was so formal and almost like she might have been trying to conceal something. But what in the heavens was it? James pondered to himself; having been involved in this mission for a while now, he knew that there was more to it than just darkness clouding her soul.

"Aha. Right. So yes, this is the perfect dominion to be away from those who you wish not to seek you out in the most clandestine of climates," James professed eagerly.

How funny that after only a minute of him saying that the rain began to hammer down even harder, smacking down onto the green grass so hard that you could hear the drops splattering on those delicate blades. Ironic that it had to rain just after Isra had come seeking her refuge. Of course, there was no other explanation. She connected with nature and the elements so well that they responded to her and whatever frame of mind she happened to be in. As one would expect with Isra being dark, the most prevailing auras of her were emotions inclined to the negative. Doubt, fear, and most importantly, anger. She also deeply desired revenge right in the pit of her heart, so naturally, what other type of weather but rain would be acceptable? Of course, it had to be tempestuous, icy showers pummeling the land with fury.

James surveyed the scene around him, noticing there was a small clearing just a stone's throw away from the picturesque Shambre Fell in the midst of a line of tall, strong pine trees that stood between Shambre Fell like a shroud. Yes, there had to be a forest habitation that sheltered this prestigious location away from prying eyes. The more James thought about it, the more he began to assume that this was a set up. That somehow Samuel and those "on high" had made it so that Isra was designated here.

Why else would this spellbound manor be put here with such fascinating rapture that only a person deeply rooted in the occult would find appealing? It didn't take a genius to work it out. Those clever folk "oh high" had put themselves in the mindset of a person tainted by the dark for a moment just to relish the anticipation of what it would be like to be led astray by things of beauty. Let's face it; if this elegant attraction was all dank and dark, saturated in centuries of cobwebs, then nobody would have gone within an inch of it for fear they'd have just found themselves knee-deep in creatures of the eight-legged variety.

However, it wasn't just Isra and James that were holed up in the humble abode of mystery. A certain raven was lurking in the grounds of Shambre Fell, sitting on top of a branch of a nearby plum tree almost falling over himself with laughter at James's predicament of not being able to understand how this was all playing out. It was safe to say that Astrid was thoroughly enjoying the show and yet you couldn't help but feel like the raven was gloating as he resiliently pointed out the facts from within his clever hiding place.

"He's been in this longer than I care to count. And yet he still challenges how it all interlocks together," Astrid mocked as he veered around the corner so he could be in the precise view of the front door of Shambre Fell. "It is really funny. I'm supposed to be the fall guy. The dense one who doesn't know what is occurring behind my back, but yet I'm so full of intelligence and wit that they can't outsmart me. But good try, boys!"

Astrid took a perched position in his prime stalking spot. Oh yes, if he was going to eavesdrop, you could bet your soul he'd ensure he wasn't observed doing so. Yes, Astrid really didn't care that yet again he had not been granted permission to dwell here like this, but the way he saw it, he was just showing Samuel and James a thing or two because he was having a real fit of rebellion now.

The raven was long tired of being ordered around and told, "Don't do this, ensure you do that or else consequences will follow!"

by Samuel and the other beings that solely worked in the light. Now he was following his own path, so to speak. And he had an idea up his claws in order to attain such anarchist privileges, soon to become the lone wolf as far as darkness versus light was concerned; Astrid was really going to turn up the heat in more ways than one. But for now, he was going to sit and keep a very close eye on James, of whom was about to get a very personal encounter with Astrid's benevolent infatuation, which of course was Isra.

"So come on, boy. Show me what you are really made of," Astrid challenged from his position as he observed James and Isra closely. He was practically goading James from his safe little perch, knowing he could mock the human as much as he wanted and James couldn't do a damn thing about it.

"Shall, er, we go in? I believe the, erm, door is unlocked," James staggered out slowly.

He had to admit he was having trouble knowing what to say to make his performance believable, but maybe with time he could work on his acting skills. After all, so much was at stake and there was only so much time left in order to form a very good impression.

"Yes. For sure," Isra replied formally.

She kept distance in her words as well as with her physical self, trailing behind James so that she was always a few steps back, keeping things dim with only one- or two-word answers, careful not to let anything out or revealing any kind of intention. One may have considered whether Isra had a hidden agenda. If James wasn't so preoccupied with knowing what to say to Isra, maybe he'd have paid closer attention to her bizarre body language. But it wasn't just Isra that James would have to be careful of, because there was a very loose cannon about to shoot off into the hemisphere courtesy of Astrid.

However, there was the small matter of what the plan was that Samuel had so meticulously devised for Isra having made it known that he was going to do something in which James would help orchestrate. It was only yesterday that they had discussed this, but James was a little blurry on some of the details. Perhaps there was something he was not remembering. A vital piece of the puzzle he'd have to fumble back into his memory to get his lapse of time back, for right now he was having difficulty recalling exactly what took place in that conversation after Samuel had said, "Good, then we have no more to discuss. Remember. Discretion in all forms."

James reached into his pockets, feeling around until he felt his fingers grasp around a cold stone. He withdrew it from his pocket and glanced at it, murmuring something under his breath as he looked down at the icy yellow tumble stone with specks of orange. The citrine was an aid to help guide one's memory when it had become lost to acts of magic.

And that was the only logical explanation as to why James was feeling flimsy in regard to what actually occurred when he and Samuel spoke intimately about his dynamic yet genius plan.

IT WAS ONLY JUST GETTING dark. James and Samuel had been sitting in Samuel's office for about an hour or so now. There were no lamps or anything exceedingly bright to guide them through it; all they had was a simple candle lit by Samuel's window which just about shed enough light for both men to view each other and scrutinize their words.

Samuel had assisted by way of making another round of two fresh and steaming hot mugs of coffee because there was going to be a lot of stamina needed for what he was about to muster in the manner of his proposal. Samuel placed James's cup on the right side of his desk before maneuvering over to his end of it and then plummeting into his soft, red velvet chair.

"There is something I have spied on during my travels. Well, sort of. I actually saw something else and made a duplicate copy in a sense. Created a place out of nothing, but put my own unique watermark on it in a manner of speaking. It's a veiled location. The irony of it is that it appears to be a wonderland, if you will. A spectrum of colors just appetizing enough to beguile any well-refined tastes. I gave it the name Shambre Fell because there is a stream guarding the enchanted tower itself," Samuel explained in a low voice. He smiled, as he was clearly impressed and pleased with himself. There was that deep feeling of satisfaction that could only be found after one had achieved something memorable that gave you that knowing that you'd done something truly amazing.

"Interesting indeed," James replied. Evidently the angelic agent had not much more to say, unsure what Samuel was leading up to or what the point in this whole creation really was and how it involved Isra.

"Yes, it is. The most important part is how we get Isra there. It is really quite sneaky on our part, I know, but think of it as killing two birds with one stone," Samuel implored. He was resolute about it; you could tell by the way his eyebrows twitched in James's direction. Samuel was hatching a very deliberate and forward plan.

James however wasn't overly convinced. He didn't comprehend what Samuel meant and felt very perplexed by it all. He too raised an eyebrow and stared Samuel dead in those shrill blue eyes of his, almost interrogating the light bringer as he piped up.

"Right, but how does Isra get to be in this revolving world of yours and how does it help us, or her? If that is even—" James spluttered as he almost choked on his coffee. The beverage was too hot and so he failed to swallow it in the way it had been designed, leading to coughing and splattering it. Not very attractive, but shocking tangents provoked such a reaction.

"I'm glad you asked, because there is a reason for everything here. One, we will know exactly where she is and be able to keep a very close eye on her. And two, she will be sheltered from the world in a very precise location where prying eyes cannot detect her. She will be under our protection, if you will, but we will not condone any reckless behavior she exhibits," Samuel professed, as it became astounding to James just how much thought had gone into this unusual yet intriguing deliberation.

A short silence filled the room as James processed this information, not looking at Samuel for a few moments while Samuel sat back on his comfortable throne awaiting James to fully consume all of which they had conversed and understand just what was ahead. Because yet again, Samuel had held back just how this clever calibration came together.

After a couple of minutes, James turned to Samuel, almost as low as whisper, and ventured, "Okay. I see your meaning behind this and yes, it is smart. But why do I get the vibe that something isn't quite as distinct as it should be here?"

The question was rogue and without merit, but someone had to bring it up because James did feel like something was being shied away from. He wasn't inaccurate on that one. Samuel veered over to the window and looked out at the scenery that surrounded his secluded yet also very beautiful world, which in turn caused James to stare out at the same imagery.

"It doesn't quite add up because what I've failed to tell you is that *you* will orchestrate her dwelling there. It doesn't matter if you don't have a hold on it all, but you will be there at the exact time that it is deemed worthy, and she will be there also. The rest you will conduct to my instruction and you will engineer Isra moving into that fortress that is Shambre Fell." Samuel took an enormous gulp of his coffee that had gone lukewarm through all the talking he had done. "Don't concern yourself with the how. Make it as though you are a misguided soul and have no knowledge of it, and the rest will face into place as it has been fated to."

Samuel motioned with a glimmering smile. It was so bright you could see the whiteness of his teeth. The light bringer was practically glowing as he sat back relaxed and carefree in his humble yet quaint abode. His plan was in motion and everything was going according to how he had designed it, right down to the letter.

The scene of being in that dark yet softly candle-lit office faded as James returned to the normality of his mind. Finding himself standing right next to Isra in the enchanted Shambre Fell, he felt as though he had only been gone for a matter of seconds. Never mind what seemed like almost an hour, as he had used the most strategic of magics just to retrieve a tiny facet that had seemingly been trapped somewhere inside his memory.

The only question that resounded now was why James would have to go to such lengths to claim back a fragile piece of his consciousness that was trapped in another dimension, so to speak? More precisely, why did James forget the events that encapsulated himself and Samuel in the first place? It was inconceivable for such a thing to commence since he had barely forgotten a single thing since his existence had taken shape in the cosmos itself. Evidently, something was amiss and plaguing his memory. The only pressing inquiry was whom, or what?

7

"Hehehe. He won't even begin to grasp the wild time I've been having while messing with his delicately formed human brain. Hahahaha!" Astrid chortled away to himself.

The raven was obviously very amused and entertained by the confusion James had experienced. Some might have said it was a step too far for Astrid, but it wasn't really likely that he'd give a shit in any case.

James was still stuck, utterly clueless as to why such vital information had irretrievably vanished from his head, but then he suddenly noticed a black silken wing sticking out of a nearby plum tree. Having an inkling, he quickly realized who that feathered wing belonged to.

James turned to Isra who was apparently bemused as to what was happening, but didn't get the chance to figure any of it out as James took over the situation promptly. "Excuse me for a moment."

Not hesitating for a second and fleetingly becoming incredibly pissed, he neglected to remember that Isra, the entire reason they were here in the first place, was right in the thick of him going absolutely mental. James snapped his fingers and froze the scene in a nanosecond. Striding over to that plum tree with his arms dangling by his sides, he was about to confront that smart ass raven or at least file some kind of investigation as to why he was down here. Again.

Ha, just what the hell does he think he's playing at? He's been told by me and Samuel repeatedly not to be anywhere near Isra, and here he is, watching the scene without a care in his feeble mind. Oh, he's in for it this time! James murmured to himself in thought as he reached the plum tree.

It was wise to note that James resisted the urge to swing his sword at the branches; while it would be enough to shake up the raven, James didn't fancy having a pecking order on his hands.

"Just what in the devil are you doing here?" James pressed Astrid firmly, noticing the raven wasn't even remotely shook up by him stomping over to the plum tree, standing and glaring at Astrid as if he were something sodden and rotten that should be squished violently.

"Oh, calm yourself. It's a free world out here! I was just stretching my wings," Astrid answered sardonically. The sarcasm in Astrid's voice was easily found as the raven didn't care at all about being discovered.

"Funny. Right here in the midst of Isra? *Again?*" he probed, now getting more irritated especially since Astrid was giving him such an attitude that James had to wonder just what side Astrid was really on. The raven was hardly acting methodical or showing concern to the cause like he used to.

James almost considered the idea that maybe Astrid wasn't really aware of what side he was on. Perhaps the raven was experiencing a midlife crisis of the spiritual variety, or something closely resembling it.

As always, Astrid showed no remorse or guilt when it came to being confronted for his misdeeds. "Yes, well. What are you going to do about it?" he challenged James with a low growl.

The noise echoed from within him so loud that one could practically sense how annoyed he was. The good advice here would have been to retreat far away before someone lost an eyeball or an equally important part of themselves, but James wasn't going to give up lightly. This whole obsession of Astrid's was really starting to grate on James's easy-going persona. It was such a simple instruction: Astrid, you can be part of our intertwined mission, but for your safety and hers, stay away from Isra at all costs. I mean, how hard is that to understand and also follow? You'd have thought Astrid would have grasped this simple concept by now. But no, he had not.

"Don't test me," James emitted, folding and placing his arms across his chest in a sullen moment in which he stared at Astrid for a few seconds.

The raven returned the awkwardness by also focusing his attention on James. Not taking in any of the other things that lie in his midst. Not looking at the greenery and the ruby-red roses or anything else that grew wildly in the natural habitat surrounding the mass monastery that was Shambre Fell. But glaring at James with such contempt that you could tell Astrid was angry regarding James. He was so foul-tempered over him that it wouldn't have been a shocker if the raven Astrid spun out of that plum tree and reached for James eyeballs. However, he didn't do that at all. Astrid kept an immense focus, almost as though he was in a deep meditation, refusing to take his eyes off the resilient James.

Someone had to break the strong-willed stance and James was the one to do it as he veered around the corner, noting that Isra was frozen in time and stood before the iconic oak door. The same one that led into the prestigious and historic tower. Isra had been awaiting James to show her around the place as he had offered to her but circumstances meant he'd had to deal with Astrid's behavior first.

"She's waiting," James called out, pointing over to where Isra was motionless and stiff as the scene stood still around her. He recognized that even her glaring neon green eyes were fixed in their sockets as well.

Astrid looked over to his left, realizing James was referring to Isra and stared at her equally as penetrative as he had with James and motioned slowly. "Yes, I see. I suppose you expect me to scamper before you awaken her?" he inquired, although it wasn't really a question as he'd expressed it in such a sardonic manner.

"That would be the desired goal I had in mind," James muttered. He was also very sarcastic since that was apparently the only way these two could successfully communicate with each other if they actually wanted a response of merit.

"As you wish," Astrid ventured softly, and without warning he soared out upward into the night sky, disappearing beneath a mass of clouds.

Astrid's actions only left James bemused as to why he had shot off like a light. Normally Astrid never paid any mind to anything anyone said to him. Something James had said or done must have triggered a reaction for Astrid to go off in a huff like that, but there was no indication what. However, the result was pleasing to James. Finally, he could resume the dramatic act pertaining to Isra with Astrid out of the picture and hopefully bothering someone who could actually tolerate his wayward antics.

"We've got much bigger matters at hand than a bird with a bee up his bonnet," James retorted as he promptly unfroze Isra.

ASTRID, however, also had bigger things in mind as he soared in and out of the gray clouds almost within reach of his destination. It was pitch black, so night had well and truly made its way across the land, but that was hardly going to deter the raven. He was going far and beyond the borders of Spirisity and Seclera put together to get to another part of the realm. Sprawnbell. A place he had not set claw in for eons and he didn't care if it took all night for him to get there because, by golly, he had business to attend to. And like most folk in the realms, it wasn't what you knew, it was *who* you knew.

Astrid had a past deeply rooted in the occult world. He knew way more things about darkness than most simple souls could comprehend. And Astrid knew better than anyone that sometimes going back to what you knew was sometimes the way of moving forward, even if it meant stirring up a bit of chaos in the process, which in this case he really didn't care for.

Just like James and Samuel, Astrid had his ways and means of dealing with things, and tonight he was going to pay a visit to an old friend to settle an old debt and unleash a few surprises their way. But like most smart-ass folk who rebelled against their supposed cause, Astrid was going to stay tight lipped about the details. Or at least until he felt the need to do otherwise. It was a scenario that would likely involve him bragging to James about how sneaky he had been and how he and Samuel hadn't been able to uncover his dodgy dealings until the very last minute.

Oh yes, I will show them. They think they hold all the cards in this mission in which light is the ultimate warrior against dark. Ha, they have no idea. Just wait until I come charging in on my chariot of hell because, oh baby, I can bring about damnation like you wouldn't believe possible! Astrid chuckled to himself in thought as he perused through the dark skies.

It wouldn't be fair to say Astrid didn't have an exact plan in mind because you don't go coursing through the skies to meet an old friend deeply embroiled in some of the darkest magics known to the realms over a tiny bit of rebellion, do you? Or maybe you do, depending on the situation, of course. However, Astrid felt his reason for going to this extreme and disappearing into the cold hard night was more than justified. He had long been tired of being told what he could and couldn't do and now he was fighting back. Only they'd never see it coming. Not the way he envisioned it.

Anyhow, a black rectangular building came into sight. A large, slacked roof dominated the rest of the enormous monstrosity of a mansion that could be seen overhead and Astrid smiled, for he knew he had reached the end of his journey. It had only taken him around two hours to arrive and it was just a little before midnight so he had made it in very good timing. Just after midnight was what was affectionately known in these parts as the witching hour, the time where rituals would take place and demonic rites, other things that weren't openly spoken about. So, Astrid's timing couldn't be any more immaculate.

Swooping downward, the raven controlled his speed, slowing

down as he needed to see which window he was going to fly into. Times had changed since he had last been present in this place so he wanted to ensure he was entering into the right one. You never know when you might accidentally fly into the wrong room and have to awkwardly explain your actions to a chambermaid as to why you happened to be in a sleeping child's room. That was never pleasant. So, it was always best to be on the lookout before you landed, just in case you weren't prepared for changes in the household. Astrid had not been to this place for eighteen years so he figured there may have been a switch around, or at least a strong likelihood of there being one.

Hmm, let's get a handle on this. Astrid pondered for a moment. *I haven't been back here for eons. And as far as I can remember, Damien always worked in a darkened room with little light, just enough to illuminate the pages of whatever book he would be poring over. So really all I need to do is seek out the light. Ha, seek the light, now isn't that ironic? All right, back to more serious considerations now, Astrid. I need to find a certain divine female who basks in the twilight. She holds the key that can unlock the part of myself that I need to really be in the thick of it.*

Astrid's meaning was a little cryptic, but he wanted to be more physically involved in this mission with Isra. Astrid felt like a teenager just at the idea of him being up close and personal with her. He was yearning to do just that. Having spent way too much time on the sidelines, not being able to touch her already made him more than willing to pay the ultimate price just to have a few sacred moments with her. Yes, it appeared as though Astrid was indeed besotted with Isra. He hadn't known much else about love except that it came with an expiration date. With Isra, he felt like she was a breath of fresh air, as though she gave new life to something the raven had long thought dead.

But first he'd have to have the ability to do so and that's where his former employers came in.

Damien Daughtry was a most prominent and greatly feared warlock that Astrid had served loyally ever since the man was a teen at the prestigious Wingdom's Academy. Of course, with his big rebellious streak when he had unleashed chaos alongside his companion Rhiannon, the academy had promptly expelled and banished him. Funny how they had recently done the same with his daughter Everilda, but yet Damien had literally ripped open the gates of Hell, allowing the ghastliest entity Rhiannon to wreak further havoc by cursing the entire female population.

Rhiannon was a demonic sorceress with more power than he could have ever imagined. But when Damien bid his goodbyes to the lively educational facility, it was no surprise that he asked Astrid to stay on with him, to be a more permanent fixture in terms of employment. Naturally, the raven accepted and the rest was made history. However, Astrid had no inclination if Rhiannon still dwelled in Damien's lair. It was an admirable thought that these star-crossed lovers would have kept it together all these years, but honestly Astrid had no clue. He was plunging into this blind, not having anything to guide him but his gut instinct, the same precious commodity that had gotten him through most of his life unharmed. He'd had many scrapes where he would have likely ended up dead or with a much worse outcome.

Astrid was still contemplating which window he was going to lunge at when suddenly down below he caught sight of a dimly lit orange flame. *Oh please, in all of Hell's glory, let that be Damien. Please let it be him that still lurks within these dingy walls,* Astrid silently prayed to himself in thought for a moment as he prepared to inspect the window in question.

The orange flame was so bright and fiery he could hardly believe it was just from a candle. That warm orange color was almost red. It was so bold and brash. Oh, maybe it was some kind of ritual candle, but in any case, he was hoping that was Damien's office. Astrid lowered his elegant form down in a sitting position as he peered into the glass. He loitered beside the window, feeling absolutely ecstatic that it was open, slightly on the latch, but still open. No words could describe how much joy was awash inside his veins knowing that his plan finally had some endurance to it.

"Fantastic. Just what I need," Astrid gushed. He was feeling incredibly proud of himself for coming this far, and thus far he had not been met with a stonewall standing in his way.

You know, it is often said that sometimes on the dark path you do find obstacles in your way, in the same way you'd find maggots crawling all over a decayed corpse. And just when you thought you'd found one part of the body where there was none, all of a sudden three or four more maggots would materialize showing how wrong you were. Blockages often masquerade themselves in one's way when they attempt to enact acts of malice. Only the strongest and determined villains succeed in defeating these things trying to deter them. Not that Astrid was a villain, but he did often rebel against that which was considered righteous and good.

Just as Astrid was squeezing himself in through that tiny space in the window, a voice called out to him.

"Hello? Who dares enter my window without my solemn knowledge?" Damien Daughtry called out. He had his arms folded across his chest and was dressed in a royal blue silk dressing gown, clearly not much for ritual in these hours as he looked as though he was ready for slumber.

Suddenly Damien gasped as he caught a glimpse of Astrid standing eagerly on the window ledge. The man's fiery yellow eyes with specks of umber were all over the raven at once as he recognized him instantly

8

———————

"My goodness! Astrid? What in god's name are you doing here, old chap? I haven't seen you in years!" Damien called out in shock. He was unable to contain his excitement over seeing his faithful companion again.

"I come in good tidings, friend," Astrid announced warmly.

You could tell how endeared he felt toward Damien. His voice was low and soft and his eyes sparkled like a warm welcoming hearth that was brightly lit. Astrid paused for a moment. Yes, it was nice and all being reacquainted with Damien, but he really should get down to business. If the lustful Rhiannon had not departed this earthly realm, Astrid was sure that his wish could be made flesh.

"Tell me; is the lady of the house still present, Damien?" Astrid inquired with a deeper, robust tone of speaking now. He tried to verbally emphasize that he had impending matters to take care of and that although it was fine to reconnect, the sheer point of his visit was that he had come to seek out Rhiannon.

Damien said nothing, which for a second made Astrid suspect that perhaps she had fallen victim to the inevitable curse that eventually capitulated most souls. But then the dark-haired fellow burst into a fit of giggles and called out, "Rhiannon? Dear, come here, for we have an honored guest."

Clearly, she had not met her demise. Astrid felt relieved at that and also quite entertained over the trick that Damien had played on him by acting so somber for a moment before he'd changed his tone. It gave Astrid great fondness to look back on his time with Damien and how much of a lighthearted man he was even when his personal life was in turmoil. Astrid had always admired that quality in Damien. It inspired him to be better. Even when life hadn't gone as you planned, you could still have a little laugh and be happy, if only for a moment before the darkness captured your soul and stole your joy.

And there a second later, the fine form that was Rhiannon appeared in front of Astrid's eyes. She was just as he had remembered. Long burgundy red hair hung past her shoulders, dangling down her back. This evening she was in an attire of a silky gray negligee with white lace trim that only complimented her deep brown, reddened eyes. They had faded over the years as they were more black in color than the last time he had witnessed Rhiannon, so perhaps she had mellowed, but nonetheless she still seemed the same. The way she walked over to Damien so slow and sensual like a goddess was enough to tell Astrid that she was still deeply embroiled in the blackened arts. And thank golly she was, because he needed her to bring him the salvation he craved more than anything.

"Ah, my exquisite angel," Damien addressed her, reaching over to grab her hand, clasping it warmly into his own. He'd always referred to her as his angel. Despite the contempt in it, it was the sweetest pet name he'd given her. Damien turned to his beloved with a fondness in his yellow-orange flame eyes he directed in Rhiannon's direction. "You remember our old fellow Astrid, don't you?" he chimed in as Rhiannon's ruby eyes glazed over the raven before lighting up as she flashed him her best smile.

"Why, yes of course. How have you been, you beautiful beast?" she canted sweetly in Astrid's ear.

Yes, Rhiannon had a bit of a thing for Astrid. It might have perturbed most household staff, but she was so loyal to Damien that Astrid knew she'd have never taken it further. She spoke so seductively and tenderly with him, but Astrid knew it was just kittenish banter. Rhiannon had always acknowledged Astrid as a beast. He never saw anything off with it, so he'd always smile and go along with it. There was no harm in her speaking to him in such an endearing way; in fact, it was safe to say he found it quite appealing. It gave him confidence in himself that another female of whom was not one of his species saw something wonderfully divine in him. It made him feel good inside, a feeling that he had not ever felt by another soul before, and so he found it rather addicting hearing that from another, enticing that feeling of pleasure that one can only feel when someone delivers unto you a most satisfying compliment that not only lifts you up but is also true.

"I am mighty fine, although my reasoning for coming here ... well, it's a little awkward actually," Astrid confessed, realizing he had drawled on a bit as he had got that sentence out there.

"Oh?" Rhiannon inquired eagerly.

Her lips were pursed and for once she was mute, staring at Astrid intently as if she was casting some sort of enchantment. He knew it was the same sort of gaze you'd give out when you were focusing on a subject that you intended to either transform into something rather revolting or destroy completely.

"I admit, I am involved with a team of folk that deal with disarming those wretched in darkness, but please believe me, I mean you and yours no harm. I come seeking something that the light believers cannot give me. I need this gift. Please understand that I have no bad intentions," Astrid recited as though he was in prayer as he seemed to plead with Rhiannon and Damien.

It probably wasn't the best action to take. He might have been seen as though he was seeking pity which, in the eyes of dark souls, would only make him seem weaker in nature. You must remember that Astrid was a strong minded and dignified fellow. He was also a deep thinker and very practical. He was a man, or should we say raven, that thought for himself and did as he saw fit. Astrid didn't bow down to the whims of anyone. He would never, ever consider himself a victim in life. He was far too aggressive in his mindset for that and always sought the silver lining in all things. He found the mere idea of wanting pity as pathetic, and quite frankly anyone that sought it from him, he would look down upon. So you can see how awkward he felt to be in this space around these souls he considered dear friends and be so lacking in masculinity, brought to almost begging them to give him something truly precious.

"Ah, yes. The love and light brigade," Rhiannon countered with a smug grin. She clicked her thumb and forefinger together with a sharp snap only to be interrupted by her beau Damien who gave her a forewarning glance.

Damien reprimanded her with a slight offish tone. "Now now, love. They have their good parts. All right, so they are rather dull and engage in all that righteousness lark. But on the whole, they just want to save humanity from toppling down into a vile hell hole that they wholly made for themselves."

He was obviously against the light for reasons that led to them banishing him, but Damien seemed to understand both sides of the coin. He was a very worldly man who had insight on both perspectives of what it was to be fully immersed in both the cruel third dimensional sphere. And then there was that place that was wicked, consuming, and unpredictable, but at least you knew where you stood there. The demonic places that one could dwell were presumed much more safer than that of the earthly precedence that so many loved to hate.

"They are so pitiful and freakish though!" Rhiannon commented with a scowl. She was obviously very much perturbed by the so-called love and light community because she had been pushed into the murkiest depths of Hell by a former lover who could not handle her femininity. Well, there's more to that story, but it made Rhiannon oh so vengeful for all time afterward.

"Yes, dear. But here now, Astrid is so much more than all those dreary individuals that gave you a hellish send-off all those years ago. He is here for our assistance and I think we should give him the assurance that we will honor his request. Whatever that may be..." Damien trailed off, carefully eyeing Astrid with a forwarding glance before turning to Rhiannon, adding, "...as he has not told us the entirety of the tale thus far."

It was in this mannerism that Damien was hinting that Astrid should carry on reciting out his wonderfully bold and hopefully exciting request of whatever had required him to travel out here all on his lonesome in such a bold extremity.

"Yes, well," Astrid said awkwardly as he tried to discard the reprimand Damien had just issued Rhiannon from his mind and move on to more important matters. "There is a mission of which the light is involved to retrieve a witch back from the darkness; however, I have vested personal interest in this and the lady herself. Her name is Isra."

Astrid articulated with broad enthusiasm as Damien listened intently. Astrid felt relieved at knowing he was finally being heard and despite the chilling atmosphere he was enveloped in, the raven was doing his best, making it a priority to ignore Rhiannon's off-putting icy looks from across the other side of the room. He could feel her venom just by him talking about the light. Pushing that to the side for a moment, he allowed it to linger before letting it fade out from his memory as he proceeded to continue telling them why he was here.

"She is prophesied to be a great being that will be responsible for much chaos being rolled out onto our dreary terrain. I have become fond of her and I wish to be more embroiled with her in the physical sense," Astrid stated clearly.

Rhiannon, who had listened to Astrid very astutely, reared her head in piquing interest before probing, "Am I to understand that you wish to be more entangled with this female?"

There was a small pause and Astrid did not answer. Not out of refusal or embarrassment, but he found it hard to admit his deep, satiating feelings that made him yearn just to be in that fair-haired maiden's midst. Damien, on the other hand, had it down completely, understanding exactly where Astrid was on this. And being a man who had been lured by the opposite sex in strange circumstances himself, Damien could see exactly what Astrid wanted.

"I think he means he'd like to be there in the vicinity with her in a more immortal way. I feel he wishes to be with her exclusively in a way no being has. Is that the right term to use here?" Damien presumed before he laid things down further. With a nod from Astrid, he continued. "He seeks her companionship but more than that. Our Astrid yearns for this dark empress of the night. He is engrossed in her. In body, mind, and soul. Wants to immerse himself in her for pure pleasure," Damien proclaimed in a bold and up-turned voice, ensuring that Astrid's intent was fully comprehended because he knew this type of predicament sorely well, having desired a creature drawn to darkness himself.

Astrid said nothing, knowing there wasn't anything he could say. After all, Damien was correct. He couldn't deny it. For once, he was realizing that he couldn't hide his indisputable attraction anymore. He was finally facing the truth that had been surging inside him for eons, taking him out piece by piece and not allowing him to rest or even hunt out a satisfying worm without being able to feel her. Think of her. He couldn't get this bewitching female out of his mind, no matter what he tried.

If you stopped and stayed still for a moment, you might have considered the idea that Astrid was under a spell, but he knew all about the occult and ways of magic. It was impossible for him to even comprehend the idea that someone could lure him to them from afar and have him under their complete will. No, he'd have never gone in for that. He wasn't the type to be fooled by magical trickery. There was no way on earth that a spell could have any effect on him since he could counteract it. It was unlikely that any kind of witchcraft could get a strong grip on him in any case. Astrid didn't really go for the soft-hearted approach. The rigidness and durability of his mind alone was way too tough for any kind of forceful enchantment to attempt or defeat, or even knock him off his guard. But Isra was enthralling to him, way more successfully than any kind of magic could. She blew his mind.

Astrid was in love with Isra but more than that he was mesmerized by what she was inside. Not the fragile creature she made herself out to be in front of her peers or the stiff, icy exterior she portrayed to everyone around her. No, he was in love with her soul. The part of her that she couldn't disguise, even if she tried real hard. Astrid saw right through it. He knew deep down who she was, internally, and that was what made him want her more than anything.

Just the mere thought of not being able to be near her was like a dagger shooting straight into his heart. More than that, it tortured every single feathered part of him more than he could bear, although it was clear in the scheme of things that Astrid was a raven and Isra was human, or she was for the moment, anyway. But he knew he wasn't supposed to develop feelings for someone that wasn't one of his own species.

He knew that wasn't the way it worked in this cruel, heart shattering world, but he also knew that you couldn't easily control these matters. When you so painfully hungered for someone and just not being able to touch them or hold them unto you, there was just no predominating it. It took over your entire body and made you lose yourself. Even if you fought it off, doing your utmost to rid yourself of those deep sinking feelings, you'd never be able to come out of it. And for Astrid, that was the reality.

He paused again, knowing that there was something here that had to give. The awkward silence between himself and Damien was bewildering, this inhibited and coarse vibe where everything felt so raw, the very place inside Astrid where yet again he struggled to find the words he needed to convey how he felt. Honesty was always a virtue of Astrid's, ever since he had been a hatchling, but now the truth was harder to discharge these days. Astrid relented, noting that nothing would be achieved until he breached the moment, and so he simply voiced, "Yes, that is more or less it," in response to Damien.

"As I thought, boy. Well, you've been an upstanding member of this household and I can't speak for my beloved here, but I think you are more than deserving of this ... gratifying desire of yours."

Damien murmured to himself through slightly closed lips for a moment. The man sat back in his robust black leather chair, clearly enriched by the lavishly intriguing conversation that was taking place in his manor on such a pleasant night. "I have to say, Astrid, old boy. A witch? I never suspected that in a thousand lifetimes."

Damien marveled in wonder at the raven. The youngish man was very much in awe of Astrid at this present time. Damien stared at the jet-black beauty as if he was something rather peculiar but yet also rare, as if this experience had given Astrid the gift of character. It was as though it had helped to shape Astrid into the man he was soon to be, in some form or another.

"Well, neither did I," Astrid piped up. "But I can promise you, she's sweet inside. I like them sweet but like most sticky, candy-coated offerings, she's got a middle where she's extra tasty. So sinful but yet so delectable to the palette." He elaborated with such passion that Damien really didn't need to hear anymore.

"I don't doubt it for a foreseeable second," Damien concurred reverently.

It was evident where Astrid stood on this indisposition of his. Some mighty wounded souls would view it as a distressing ailment in which Astrid was the victim, but that wasn't how he saw it at all. Astrid knew this was a profound, inexplicable connection in which he was being shown the true gift of love and all its faults, rolled into one generous, foil-zipped package. And perhaps it would be challenging along the way, but the way Astrid had it figured he was going to swoop down and capture his prize in the end. Love would have to win out, otherwise he was doomed to feel something for an eternity and not ever lay claim to it. That would be tragic indeed.

"Anyhow, Rhiannon, dear?" Damien turned to his beautiful demoness with a smile before requesting in an eager voice. "Do you think we can deliver Astrid's greatest wish?"

Rhiannon glanced up at her engaging beau with a wicked glint in her eye. The smile she had plastered across her ruby red lips where she elegantly bit her lip, flashing her shiny white teeth only showed she was more than ready to cooperate. "I see no reason as to why we cannot. But what can our darling boy do for us in return?" she asked as she rubbed her forefinger and thumb together in a sensual manner. It was almost like she was expecting something on command, a little tantalizing feat that would be the most encompassing reward for her immorally necromantic efforts.

Astrid's head dropped. *Oh golly, I didn't predict that. I thought maybe we could have a quiet, adult discussion and it would be, hey presto, in the sense of me saying it in my new physically robust human form. I never saw any bartering involved. Now this is a pickle and a half,* Astrid conversed with himself mid thought.

However, Damien's reaction caused Astrid to look upward again, for the man did not like what his charming entity had said. He seemed angry at his love. It was as though he was criticizing her. Like he wasn't impressed with her saying there should be some sort of price. As though he expected that she would do this deed freely because Astrid had been a loyal servant of theirs for a long time. And as far as Damien was concerned, no payment was needed. Damien said nothing but it was clear he was riled by Rhiannon's gesture. His expression could only mean sheer annoyance of what she was proposing, but then Rhiannon suddenly looked sad, and Damien caught on fast.

His wicked enchantress of sorts was never sad. Never in all her immortality. Okay, so she might have cried a few tears when she had been plunged into the murkiest depths of Hell, but that was lifetimes ago. What could possibly trigger such an emotional tidal wave of emotions that his darling girl looked as though she was about to break down into a somber rage which was unusual for someone that was normally so self-contained?

"What is it, dear?!" Damien called out to his lover in a softened tone. He showed concern for her but couldn't understand why she was downtrodden in the beginning of what looked like some sort of sinister depression.

Rhiannon glanced at Astrid for a solid second before facing Damien, dead-eyed so she could almost penetrate his golden-orange sheened eyes with one stare. It was hard for her to communicate emotionally since that wasn't really her forte, but on this occasion she'd made the exception. Being a demonic entity that rested entirely on the idea of bloodlust and causing havoc in the form of pain and sorrow and more besides, Rhiannon wasn't exactly the lady you'd expect to find in floods of tears.

Creatures that originate from the world of the damned have no feeling inside them, no empathy whatsoever because it doesn't exist in that realm. It just doesn't have any bearing on what these beings do. It doesn't matter whether that's ripping someone's spine out and watching them squirm while they suffer a hapless death, slowly reduced to a quivering mess before they eventually depart this mortal plane. Or if it was having somebody restrained and chained up to a stone wall while teasing them with hot molten lava bubbling away only inches from their feet, ready to rise up and shower them with its scalding fury.

Rhiannon shrugged what looked like the remnants of a tear from her face before addressing Damien solemnly with a forlorn look that was also very fleeting as she spun her head around so fast, that if she was human it would have likely come clean off. Just like that. But of course, Rhiannon didn't have any trace of a soul in her. She could twist and twirl her elegant hourglass frame however she pleased without a single speck of damage being done to her physical self. Demons were built with this ability.

"It's nothing, honestly." She paused through a momentary silence before facing the both of the males in the room that stood before her. "Well actually, I was just thinking about *her*." Rhiannon emitted a small half smile as her face seemed perkier in color. Her cheeks seemed to have lit up almost resembling her ruby red lips just not as blaring and brash.

"Her?" Astrid pressed.

He felt confused for not knowing just whom Rhiannon was speaking of. However, it appeared that whoever it was, they were very near and dear to Rhiannon to have her in such a state of despondency. Rhiannon's gaze tumbled to the floor as if she had sunk into a well of desperation before rising up, redder than ever and showcasing either rage or fury; it was hard to fathom which one it was before she erupted almost catastrophically,

"Her! As in my earth-bound daughter, Everilda. She comes of age this year. I haven't seen her. Ever," Rhiannon divulged, almost to the point where she might have collapsed. The stronghold of the peaking emotion was sending her into a blurred frenzy of anguish as she said it.

"Everilda?" Astrid gasped, unable to believe what he'd just heard.

NO! It was impossible. Inconceivable even, for it to be the very same one. Astrid rebuffed it at once as he considered it inside his head space. Was it possible that Everilda, the witch that had just been recently relinquished of her immortality, was also the long-lost daughter of Damien and Rhiannon? The exact same girl that had cruelly betrayed the sanctity of Isra's darkened heart?

My goodness, isn't it amazing how everything is connected? All these lives are intertwined in the most baffling way and none of them have any knowledge about it. Won't that be a feat when they discover just how pertinent with one another they really are? Astrid guffawed to himself, almost dying inside laughing at the mere idea of such a thing.

Astrid's usual position in these situations was to offer some words of comfort and reassurance but as soon as he'd heard that all too familiar word "Everilda," he found he could suggest nothing but the revelation that would soon bring Rhiannon to her knees.

"Everilda, eh? I know her. She's just been made mortal courtesy of Wingdom's Academy." Astrid blurted the truth out without a moment's pause before he added without hesitation, "She's the former best friend of Isra. The woman I seek to become more abreast with."

Rhiannon's hair practically stood on end. You could see the straight cut burgundy red hair fixed his motion as her blood red eyes were fastened on Astrid, not moving a muscle or stopping to breathe as her mind and heart united. She was left reeling at what she had just heard.

"Really?" She gasped, clasping her hands onto her mouth as she watched Damien's reaction. Naturally, being a warlock and more modest, showing even less emotion than her, Damien was much more composed in situations like this.

All he said in response to Astrid's revealing insight was, "Interesting indeed." But his response soon quickly turned to an interrogation and then more swiftly on, a criticism. "My daughter has lost her ability to perform the magics, why am I not shocked at this? Goodness, gracious. I dare not to dwell on what caused such a reaction from the esteemed institute of prejudiced dimwits," he muttered a little too sneeringly.

"Yes, she tried setting up another student for a misdemeanor. The academy found her out to be a prevaricator," Astrid answered openly without delay.

He wanted to ensure he was giving unto them all the facts. They weren't likely to be able to source it from anyone else but him since they had no contacts within the human world. "But Everilda's punishment was so severe as she did her utmost to make them believe that this student, Isra to be precise, was in actual fact, engaging in dark magics. Hence why her tainted gifts were taken from her and she was promptly banished," Astrid explained while also doing his best not to offend either Rhiannon or Damien, as both had history with the prestigious Wingdom's Academy.

Damien mouthed sullenly, "Well, at least she has something in common with her father."

Rhiannon didn't care much for her eternal partner's insult of their daughter, but she did have other ideas on how to make this arrangement work more into her favor. She ignored Damien's harsh judgment before swiftly looking up at Astrid, eyeing him with ease as she inquired, "Do you think you could introduce me to my daughter, or maybe just tell me of her whereabouts?"

Astrid smiled at her with a wink as he perused the idea, only to give a very sharp-witted response. "That I can do. It's likely dangerous and most quite forbidden, but I find I am engaging more and more in practices that are taboo. At least the ones pertaining to me, anyhow." He elaborated with a snigger before returning his attention back to

Rhiannon. He focused his beady yellow eyes on her before asking, "Will you make me a man?"

It wasn't strictly a request but more a statement as he sat perched awaiting his newfound freedom that would soon be a reality.

"I can make you what you desire to be. But please keep watch on my daughter. I ask so very little but that in payment for your desire to become flesh personified" Rhiannon instructed him.

"Yes, by all means, make sure she doesn't make another sorry hazard of her life," Damien interjected behind them.

Neither Rhiannon or Astrid found much hilarity in his remark, but Astrid focused on one thing only: to be a human, although the idea of it, he had always detested since he had much contempt for humans, but he knew this was the only way he could be with Isra. In the flesh, literally. Nothing else would matter to him now except this one small thing.

"Rhiannon, dear. Do your thing," Damien stated calmly, having collected himself after hearing that his daughter was a complete and utter failure.

"All right," the demoness replied before closing her eyes in rapturous concentration. Raising a finger to her lips while her eyes were motionless told both men that they were to be silent for the duration of this. She began dancing in a very sultry and enchanting manner, her hips gyrating and sinking to the floor with her knees as she was engrossed in a trance that no man dared breach.

Before long, she raised her arms and then green glimmering energy traveled over to Astrid, encapsulating him in its invisible arms before transporting him beside Rhiannon. There the energy peaked and surged, growing more fiery, glowing like rapid green flames as it surrounded Astrid like a cage. Those feisty luminous green flames completely covered him with their warmth, not allowing anything to get in or out of the energetic field they had made. Suddenly the energy dispersed, and Rhiannon opened her eyes, only too pleased to be staring at the product of her handiwork.

In place of Astrid's jet-black covering was now a robustly handsome and tall humanized fellow staring back at her with golden yellow eyes. Only too happy to look at his fine form as he examined himself, Astrid noted how long his legs were in replacement of his once sharpened claws. And now instead of feathers in the shade of onyx, Astrid had a fine mass of gray hair covering the top of his humanized head, distinguished by some very distinct silver specks. His entire body was something to be proud of.

The former raven could only marvel in amazement of himself as he retorted with an amused gibe, "Okay, now I'm really in a position to show those light bringers a thing or two."

9

Astrid admired himself again, preening at his silvery gray hair that dominated the top of his head.

He was only too happy to be showing such a full mass of hair as he had expected his transformation to have the odd glitch or two, but no. He was a fine specimen of a man. Tall, rigid and muscled in all the right areas. Astrid was ecstatic with his appearance and didn't even mind the grayness! After all, he was a good few centuries old, having very recently turned two hundred and twenty-two. But an immortal never boasted about his age. It wasn't considered good practice. And since he was a raven, it was hardly noticeable on him anyway.

Astrid was in good spirits, however. Now in a physical meat suit and able to roam around as he pleased, there was one particular destination in mind, but what he didn't bank on was James. For he was currently showing Isra about the historic Shambre Fell tower now.

JAMES HAD FORGOTTEN that while he had delved back into his memory, it had been a few seconds and Isra was standing right next to him, perplexed as he seemed to be lost in the midst of a deep thought. Unapologetically stood there, holding some yellow crystal in his hand was all Isra could make out, but she was curious. Feeling like she had been waiting long enough and extremely impatient, she jolted him with a sharp tap on his shoulder.

"Oh, er..." James stuttered, not expecting the knock. "I am sorry, I seem to be..."

He stopped before he finished that last word as he knew he couldn't tell her where he had really gone. He was supposed to act like a human. That meant also behaving like one and not drifting off to dimensions lost in fragments of time.

"Missing in action?" She finished the sentence for him, seeming quite annoyed, for she had been conversing with this man for a while now and nothing was really moving ahead. Isra wanted to get a real good look at this tower although she had no clue whatsoever as to why. There was just something alluring about it. Something that had drawn her over here. *That's bizarre. I don't even remember why I came here. Oh goodness, perhaps I am losing my mind.*

Isra pressed a fingertip to her lips as she pondered as to why she was here in the first instance. It gave her great difficulty remembering what brought her here. And that was unusual because her mind was always so clear. If Isra was at all paranoid, she may have considered the notion that she was under a spell. But she wasn't.

"Yes. That is the gist of it," James answered her, totally shaking Isra from out of her mindful bubble. "Where were we?" James asked as both he and Isra stood against the elegant brown ochre oak door.

He had been here for ages now and a lingering fate of entering this entrancing manor was dawning upon them both for long enough. James had to admit, he was intrigued to know just what was to be discovered inside those hollow walls. This fantastical creation that Samuel had conjured up out of nothing. The fascination only continued to pull him with interest as he stared at the ornate golden doorknob. Taking the first step, he wrapped his hand around it, twisting it. A small clicking sound emitted as the door unfastened and was pushed open.

As he wanted to be a gentleman, James held it open for Isra as she breezed past him and let herself in. He followed suit, trailing softly behind her.

Now that both James and Isra were inside, there was nothing left to do except explore this sensational chateau. James imagined there would be a lot of bold flavor beautifully depicted with dark colors and breathtaking decor that would make you feel as if you were in an enthralling yet magical realm. He wasn't wrong. The brashness of his prediction hit them as they were faced dead on with scarlet red wall covering and in the midst of it a grand stone and marble staircase. Twenty or so steps all perfectly aligned with each other that presumably led to another level of this magnificence of a residence.

"After you," James offered to Isra as he gave her precedence to go up the stairs as her wandering green eyes were equally as curious as James to know just what they might find up there.

It was her that trolled on ahead to yet another majestic oak door that Isra pushed open without hesitation only to find herself gazing at plain walls surrounded by a mass of gold. Her first impressions were that this was some kind of room you'd expect to find royalty. There was an elegant red armchair facing the back wall that was also dressed with ornate gold finishing. This only contrasted the luxury red velvet that was all over the seat and the arms of the comfortable chair. Yes, it passed as that when Isra couldn't resist sitting down upon it, resting her back against the soft material. Her eyes traveled up the ceiling as she lost all her cares for a moment, feeling like she was a queen, being idly sitting in this chair, losing all connection with the world, if only for a moment.

It was nice. She could easily imagine herself here which was baffling as Isra still didn't know what she was doing here. Being led astray by this profound yet intriguing dark-haired fellow and not sure whether she should follow him or not, just in case she ended up in a rabbit hole and tumbled down into chaos. But at least that was the way she was envisioning it in her head.

"You found it then?" James muttered, startling Isra in her trance as she lowered her eyes until they found him immediately setting upon them as she regained her composure. "It suits you," he added with a smile, uneasy as to whether he had offended Isra as she wasn't giving him a response.

Isra's behavior was even more enigmatic to James as she lifted herself from the red seat without delay and turned away from him and allowed her eyes to gaze at the plain black walls that seemed to dominate this enormous beast of a throne room. Almost in a meditative state, she placed a hand upon the cold stone wall, feeling the energies of all who had dwelled here before.

"Yes, I could see myself in here," Isra replied with a sharp twang emitting from her lips.

It was almost as though she was half considering the idea and resenting it at the same time. For some reason she felt off at the fact that James' guy had led her inside here and still she couldn't comprehend as to why this had come about.

What was I doing before I found myself in this wilderness? That I cannot recall. It must have been some whimsical daydream that hit like a light. It's so baffling to me. I don't know who this man is and yet I let him drag me on yonder. If I was my usual self I'd have politely declined and gone on my merry way by now. But yet I stay. How peculiar, Isra thought to herself as James smiled at her.

To be truthful she found him a little over friendly. Why did humans have to be all nice anyhow? I mean, what was the point in it unless they were making a vain attempt to gain something. I mean really what was the purpose? No, Isra much preferred to be honest at least if she wasn't being that tactful, it was guaranteed to be raw. And not false. Isra really detested that whole facade in which a person would be so lovey dovey fake with somebody when in reality they couldn't stand to be in the same universe as them. Just be honest. Say what you feel. And to hell with what they think. That was her forte.

With James however, it wasn't that she felt he was being fake with her. No, there was something about him that led her astray, almost like he was holding a lantern with the path brightly lit by a thousand fireflies and she was compelled to follow. Weird, as she didn't know him at all, having only just met less than an hour ago. And the mere idea of it was discomforting to her. She was used to running the show. Having things her way. So, the even bare-boned meaning that someone might hold the power over to do that was really unsettling to say the least.

How would you feel if you had all your metaphorical ducks in a row, everything neat and just the way you liked it and suddenly something came along and threatened to rip it all to pieces? I doubt you'd be too happy about that. That was Isra's exact feeling. The fear of not wanting to change because everything was just to her liking right now.

She had no intention of playing for the good guys. She was far too complacent in the role of dark warrior that she had going for herself. Nothing else would even remotely hit a notch on her radar while she had that vibe going. But Isra figured that James was likely one of those human souls that were so determined they would stop at nothing to get what they wanted in the end. That bugged her a little. Because although she knew very little about this human, Isra did know that something else was at work here and she was slightly unnerved and also curious about it. Just like Alice in the way she would jump into the rabbit hole not knowing where she'd end up.

"Yes, so can I," James murmured loud enough so she could hear him.

Funny he talks the talk, but can he walk the mile? Isra wondered to herself. "So, what brings you over this neck of the woods anyway?" Isra inquired. She felt bold and spirited. And there was a yearning inside her to know more about this individual although the circumstances of how she had met him were rather bizarre. However, something deep in Isra's soul told her there was more to James than he was letting on.

"I'm just visiting for a while," James spouted out.

Okay, he and Samuel hadn't rehearsed this part of the plan. He barely even knew the foundations of it except that he had to play along. What did that even mean anyway? Just let it flow, he could hear Samuel saying.

Yes well, it was easy for you since you are not in the presence of her. One wrong word and she could zap me into oblivion. James cursed to himself in thought. *That damned raven better not mess up any of this either. Always up to no good with his irritating little schemes. Stalking her because he's so obsessed and then playing the part of the victim when he's caught red handed. Who does he think he is? I tell ya, he really needs taking down a notch or two. But for now, he better stay out of my way or I may not be wholly responsible for my actions.*

"I, umm, I have family ties here." James lied through gritted teeth.

Yes, he really needed to work on this shit better. Who knows if he was fooling Isra. He sure as hell wasn't convinced but he had to say something to keep the energy flowing between them. One tiny mistake and all could be lost. Nobody would want that. And fuck having to explain to Samuel why his grand plan spectacularly bombed out of nowhere. Nope, James did not want that responsibility.

It was better to weave a few tales for now until he knew exactly what Samuel had in mind. After all, he was the instigator of this. James was just carrying out his orders. Who knew what kind of ideology Samuel had in mind pertaining to Isra? It was a case of sitting back and awaiting instructions because nobody was really in charge of this matter except the light bringer himself.

"Oh. I don't have any family here. To be truthful, they've long surpassed me some years ago," Isra confessed with a bittersweet feeling. The memory of her family was pungent and grotesque and she had no desire to reclaim her history in any means but yet again this mortal was bringing this stuff out of her.

"I'm sorry to hear that," James professed. He gave it a sympathetic edge to show there was some genuine feeling about it and of course, himself. He certainly didn't want to come across as one of those peasants that was so cold hearted that they barely even noted how others felt.

"It is no matter," Isra recited calmly. "I am long past it. So, this place?" She took her hand away from the wall and eyed James dead in the center of him. "Has it been unoccupied for a long time?" Isra questioned with a feverous glow in her eyes. Yes, she was curious. There was no doubt there.

"I feel it has been empty for many years now," James proclaimed efficiently, "but I would have to confer with my master back in our land. Hey, here's an interesting twist; why don't you come with me? You can hang in the gardens while I get talkative and find out the answers you are seeking," James suggested to Isra.

James wasn't sure if she'd go for it, but this was a good plan. Isra didn't just need her return on the past of this mystical chateau, James needed to know exactly what to say to her. He didn't want to be the one that had to plead with Samuel when all hell broke loose upon this mortal world. Just because somebody happened to say the worst possible thing to a female that could potentially plunder them all into chaos. I mean, that really would be most disappointing to Samuel's ears.

"That sounds like it would be something," Isra mused to him in a quiet voice. "But won't someone else occupy this humble abode while we are gone?"

"No, certainly not. Hardly anyone around these neighboring woods has the knowledge of this location's mere existence. I highly doubt someone would come along and set up camp in there," James retorted with a slight hint of sarcasm. *Oh, maybe that wasn't quite the right thing to say, but never mind,* James mumbled to himself in a mid-thought. "So, you shall accompany me to the majestic realm of Spirisity?" James stated to Isra, almost imploring in her direction.

"It really does sound intriguing, I must say. All right, dear boy, I shall go with you. I'll make friends with the inhabitants of the land while you get chatty with the folk in charge," Isra said as if she knew how the system worked which was funny as the realm of Spirisity was a closely guarded secret to those who did not encounter it.

"Oh, the trip is one way, in the sense we will be there in a flash or two!" James chuckled toward Isra.

And just as her lips were about to emit some kind of fancy retort,

James clicked his thumb and index finger, sending a rush of shiny gold light all around them.

The second after, they stood next to a tall gray castle-like building amongst masses of green and yellow. The crocuses were in fine form considering it was almost winter. Spouting their fine yellow ochre heads with the petals flowing freely around them. They were so bold and bright that they stood out amongst all the green pasture that dominated Spirisity, giving the location a real nature vibe. Little delicate violets were equally spread around the grassland, giving it that old grand vintage countryside feel. It was somewhere you could imagine yourself in when you wanted to sit outside on a warm summer's day. A quaint little spot located in the middle of nowhere, in which one could sit and relax, forgetting all the things that lay beyond this beautiful garden.

But they weren't here to admire the scenery. At least James wasn't anyway. He figured he could leave Isra unattended for a few moments while he conversed with Samuel because he really needed to be brought up to speed on all facets of the plan. Whatever that was.

James excused himself with a small cough, turning to Isra with a friendly stare as he motioned forward to her, "Erm, I don't mean to be rude, but I really have to go and talk to my boss. You'll be all right here for a few moments?"

"I see no reason why not," Isra replied.

"Okay, no problem. I'll get chatty with the man of the manor, but I'll be back," James said to her in an assertive manner, quickly turning to the bold brass iron gates that guarded the interior of Spirisity from any onlooker before pushing past them, disappearing beyond it and leaving Isra unoccupied in the serene green mass of arcadia.

10

Isra found herself lured by the vibrant veracity of a bright violet as an unsuspecting soul watched her from behind the vast mass of overgrown bluebells poking their heads out eagerly.

"That's right boy, you run along to old daddy." Astrid scoffed from his hiding place as his bold yellow eyes kept their focus on Isra. Having only been standing here for five minutes and witnessing Isra and James arrive, Astrid had been waiting for James to scamper off before he could get real close with the lady in question. "So, let's see what our girl is really made of. Let's catch her attention with something wonderful to behold. A beautiful beast of a creature that enchants the whimsy inside her blackened heart."

Astrid closed his eyes. He was obviously in deep concentration because he said nothing, keeping a strong hold on his breathing ensuring it was rapid and both shallow at the same time. It was the powerful way one would achieve oneness with themselves and also be in a consciousness beyond any kind of mortal comprehension. The place you'd be in where you were completely relaxed and also in control of your bodily actions. The only true way to succumb to real forcefulness is by being at peace with yourself. Astrid was a real master at that.

It was only for a minute and then Astrid opened his eyes as a robust black unicorn stood before Isra, chewing on some grass while neighing a little. Just enough to grasp the witch's attention.

"Oh my, you are a beauty of a soul, aren't you?" Isra cooed in the animal's direction. "Where did you come from, sweet thing?" Isra asked the creature as she stood upright, proceeding to make her way over to the magnificent beast that had her all aglow. It was as though she had never laid eyes on something so

"That ought to do it." Astrid chuckled.

He watched closely as Isra suddenly lifted her head and took her focus away from the violet flower she had been admiring. It was magical with her eyes falling onto the gorgeous black unicorn that was ranked up before her. This divine jet-black colored animal had such a splendidly pleasing form with beautiful white dazzling eyes to match it.

"Oh, we are in business!" Astrid chortled, doing his utmost not to burst out into spontaneous laughter. He watched as Isra approached the graceful black being and gently reached over for its head, rubbing his nose softly as she nuzzled him. "And that, my friends, is how to lure a girl. Tempt her dark willful self with something equally as lurid but also oh so seductive and pleasant on the eyes while also taking care to enthrall her darkened heart."

The raven turned man looked incredibly pleased with himself as he displayed the most smug, wicked grin as he licked his lips eager to unleash the next installment of his mayhem.

"Oh, they made a big mistake when they shut me out because now I'm the one meddling with their prestigious operation," Astrid joked quietly to himself.

Samuel sat idly at his desk. His eyes were half closed almost in a meditative state or one of deep contemplation. A glass of whiskey was positioned in his right hand and his other one was comfortably

resting upon the arm of his red velvet chair. Imagine how startled he was when the door flew open at a moment's notice.

James burst in, staring at Samuel in his slightly dozy state, noting that the light bringer had been drinking.

"Good heavens, James. Couldn't you have knocked?" Samuel shot at him with annoyance, dusting himself off as he was clearly so rudely disturbed without notice.

"Sorry, I didn't realize you were having a private moment, old man!" James sniggered.

He carefully observed the open whiskey bottle that was nearly halfway finished. The robust entity sat on the shelf behind Samuel with the lid slightly unfastened. Samuel had obviously been helping himself to more than one serving of the glorious brown sticky liquid beverage. Samuel glared at James, huffing as he waved a prodding finger at him.

"Very amusing I am sure, young fellow!"

Yes, it didn't seem like Samuel was best pleased with James's statement as he immediately launched into what might have come across as a hissy fit versus a polite reprimand aimed in James's direction. Still waving his finger at James, Samuel scolded him.

"I'm not an old man and secondly, where have you been? Come. Sit," he ordered, pointing at the empty chair next to his desk.

James sat, only eyeing Samuel, for he seemed a little out of sorts. The light bringer swiftly lifted himself from his arm chair, extending his arm and reaching for the large bottle of fine Irish whiskey. Also, he grabbed another glass tumbler off the shelf and placed it in front of James, who looked incredibly baffled when Samuel poured him a glassful of the stiff drink before replenishing his own with the delightful sickly liquid.

"It's a little early for me," James rebuffed him, pushing the glass away from him.

Samuel gave James a hardened stare, pushing the glass of whiskey backwards again. "Nonsense! Drink with me. It's not a suggestion. That's an order. Besides, after what I am about to tell you, I feel like we will both need one." Samuel grunted before taking a huge swig of his fanciful beverage.

"You've heard from Astrid then?" James piped up.

"No," Samuel retaliated. There was a hint of anger and irritation in his voice. A husky long drawn-out growl emitted from him as he waited to see what would come next.

The whiskey still seemed like a remarkable idea because now Samuel was pondering that he would need to be half-cut in order to properly take in the revelation of whatever mania James would be detailing him in regard to Astrid. In all fairness, Samuel hadn't seen the raven for a while and was beginning to wonder what he was up to, but with James sitting here about to tell all, Samuel figured he didn't have to marvel over it for much longer.

"What has he done now?" Samuel groaned. He uttered a huge sigh as he finished the rest of his drink before slamming the glass back down on the desk. His eyes moved over to the bottle in front of him, tempting him wildly to pour himself another, but Samuel found by pushing the bottle away from him, he still had some restraint.

The light bringer felt like whatever he was about to hear wouldn't be good. So it was best to be prepared for the worst in Samuel's mindset. With the state he was in at the moment there was no positivity to be found anywhere. He was drained from this whole rescuing Isra from darkness mission, or at least they were doing their utmost to try to, anyhow. And the forlorn man was honestly considering giving up and just admitting defeat to the demonic foes they had fought so hard not to lose against.

Yes, it sounded silly and really hypocritical for Samuel to be in such a tizzy, but his patience was wearing thin. Astrid swanning off whenever he pleased wasn't really helping matters and goodness knows what that naughty raven was getting up to behind the scenes. It was obvious to anyone that Samuel was stressed, but you wouldn't have thought he would be the type to fall down so easily. He seemed such a strong-willed type of guy that wouldn't succumb to defeat but maybe years of fighting the spiritual warfare against those who switched from the light were beginning to take its toll at last.

He wasn't exactly looking like a fresh-faced maiden the last couple of days. His jet-black slicked hairline was constantly receding and those blue eyes of his were more sullen than bright, but possibly from the constant indulging in his favorite tipple. And let's face it; Samuel really did like his whiskey. Not to mention both his men in charge had gone missing in action. First James had scampered off to who-knew-where for eons, and then Astrid was hardly around anymore. Always off somewhere and never really filling Samuel in on it, so Samuel was left to fester and it became somewhat of a habit. Looking at him, maybe he just needed a good long sleep but perhaps some positive news would also be very welcoming also.

"He hasn't done anything," James murmured before also taking a swig of his whiskey.

The taste obviously wasn't to his liking as James pulled a face as though he was about to vomit. Evidently, he wasn't as hardcore with the stronger variety of spirits as was the refined Samuel. Still, it gave the light bringer a chuckle which brought a rarely seen smile to his face.

Thank the lord for small mercies, Samuel joked to himself in thought. *Because the last thing I need is a runaway that's got a screw loose about to cause more havoc in my domain.*

"But I have done something and I am not sure if you will be pleased with it," James said quietly.

He was anxious, Samuel could tell. The way James was twiddling his fingers and thumbs in such a rhythm was enough to indicate he was worried about what the spiritual old man would say. Not that Samuel was old, but James had already made that assumption once this evening. Samuel had not been too happy being told he was getting on in years even though that exact phrase hadn't been used. He still took a dislike to it because even light bringers that looked young and handsome still got touchy over things such as their age.

Samuel was the first to break the ice since James wasn't letting on to what it was that was either about to send Samuel insane or put him at ease; Samuel presumed it would be closer to him losing his sanity.

"Good heavens, what have you done, boy?" Samuel interrogated James with a furrowed brow. His frown lines were more prominent than usual.

James was sure that he was able to count at least ten, but it was already established that Samuel was perilous with his own troubles of the shadowy world.

"I've brought Isra over to Spirisity. She's in the gardens," James admitted with a lower than normal voice, like he was trying to maintain a calm atmosphere since Samuel was already on tenterhooks awaiting the worst.

"You've done what?!" Samuel shrieked, banging his fist upon his desk, displaying his fury. "Fucking hell, James, where is your head? She's a witch! And this is a sacred realm. One of which is doing its absolute best to prevent types like her from getting in. Fuck me! Is it me, or are you all going bonkers of late, hmm?"

Samuel launched into a tirade, seeming as though he was referring to Astrid as well but it was unclear as he was raving like a lunatic. In any case, Samuel may as well have been talking to himself in his heavy rant as James zoned out, standing up and walking over to the window where he was keeping a very close eye on Isra. And with one quick glance, James noted that she was still there and not causing any issues so he breathed a sigh of relief; however Samuel was still not amused.

"Well, she's just outside. I said I wouldn't be long," James explained, trying to win back some good favor from the forlorn Samuel.

"I suppose you are right," Samuel relented softly. "But seriously, next time, consult me first! Isra is not supposed to be anywhere near this place! All right, I know I brought her here, but be that as it may. It could jeopardize so many lives if she was to get wind of our operation, do you hear me?" Samuel seemed to have calmed down a little. "Anyway, let's have another drink," he muttered, reaching over for the whiskey bottle.

Only it appeared that James had other ideas besides a heavy drinking session.

"Haven't you had enough already?" he asked Samuel bravely. Bold enough to probe into Samuel's private business was one thing, but prying into that of someone who was also his boss? Oh dear, that was murky territory indeed.

"Do you still want to be employed in the morning?" Samuel pressed James with a stern look.

It was hard to tell whether Samuel was being serious or whether he was just having a joke. But the look in those fierce looking sky-blue eyes of his was one that said, "Don't fuck with me, I'm not playing today," and James sure as hell didn't want to find out what that meant.

"Erm, I only meant..." James started.

"Oh, don't be such a wet flannel. Have a drink with me! And then you will go and collect your witch because no doubt she's getting bored with us chattering away like sparrows." Samuel snickered with glee as he eagerly poured both himself and James a tall glass of whiskey. Now the bottle was completely done in, so Samuel discarded it on the window ledge before handing James his glass. "Oh, and she's *your* problem now. I need a vacation from all this crazy chicanery!"

Samuel guffawed as James accepted his glass reluctantly.

"No problem," James acknowledged, as he veered away from the window, just literally about to sit down when suddenly Samuel happened to catch sight of something as he gazed out of the window into the open space that surrounded his fantastical realm.

He almost dropped his glass in amazement as he saw the most auspicious thing: a black unicorn stood next to Isra as she fussed over the creature tenderly stroking its long, black mane. And black really shone out against all the greenery.

Taking a step back and facing James before opening his mouth, Samuel voiced carefully, "Tell me, James; since when did black unicorns happen to dwell in Spirisity? I am dying to know!" Samuel derided in a sardonic tone although it was apparent he was asking a very direct question.

James looked taken aback as Samuel stood in front of him so

sullenly that James feared the light bringer might actually implode. He'd had to endure so much already. Who knew how much more he could possibly take before completely losing his mind?

"What do you mean, a black unicorn?" James questioned, looking worried and also very perplexed. Black unicorns were considered to be creatures of the purest darkness and of course were not given entry into Spirsity. So how one got in would be anyone's guess but whatever it was, it couldn't be anything good.

"What do I mean? I'll show you what I fucking mean! Right there! A black unicorn being pampered and fussed over by our little witch in question!" Samuel exclaimed at such a high-pitched tone that James had to put his hands across his ears to stifle out the noise.

Before he made his approach to the window to see for himself what Samuel was referring to, Samuel pointed his finger at the unicorn, waving his hands unnecessarily. It was clear to all and sundry he was pissed off.

"See! There." Samuel jeered. "I'm not imagining it. I know my own eyes even when I've had a few whiskeys. And that, my boy, is a black unicorn. Question is, how the hell did it get into my land, hmm?"

James was now standing by the window ledge peering out and he saw it immediately. Isra was still on her own, in the case of human company anyhow, but she was all over this exquisite being that absolutely had her full attention, preening over the delightful soul as it enchanted her with its brilliant white eyes and silky soft jet-black fur. It was safe to say Isra was in awe of the majestic animal that was in her presence.

If only James had paid more attention, he might have caught sight of the crafty Astrid who was still peeking from behind the bluebells in his newly made human form, cleverly disguised behind nature's own art as he watched Isra become fascinated with his creation. The beautiful black unicorn that he made appeared out of thin air, well actually there was more to it than that but a good warlock never revealed his secrets.

As it turned out, Rhiannon had bestowed Astrid with some of her magics, but Astrid already had some of his own to behold, the dark horse he was. Oh yes, Astrid had the ability to conjure up any old thing he wanted, having been descended from a long line of ravens fully immersed in the occult, but he didn't go around shouting that stuff out. He was more the quiet type. Sneaky and resilient and would only resort to such trickery when he deemed the situation to be just.

Samuel uttered a sigh, feeling once more defeated. He was repugnant as he sunk flat into his red velvet armchair, tapping his fingers merrily on his desk as if he was anticipating more revelations. It was also evident that the last past of Samuel's rant was a line of inquiry, but James didn't have the answers Samuel sought out. More to the pity as Samuel grew more and more irate by the second.

"I see it. Yes. Hmm. I have no idea how it materialized there," James responded to Samuel sharply.

James took due care to not only be swift but making sure he was not ignoring the spiritual warrior that looked more and more despondent as time went on. Just one mistake could really send Samuel tumbling over the edge. It had been a tough few days and now more and more things were occurring that were likely to send him bat shit crazy and nobody would want that.

"Hmm. Nobody seems to know anything. Well, that, my boy, is a black unicorn and they are not welcome in my realm! It wasn't there until you dragged your witch over here for whatever fun and games you brought her here for, so I suggest you go down there and find out what's up before I actually go insane!" Samuel commanded as he reached for his whiskey bottle, only to be disappointed as he remembered it was empty.

"Right you are. I shall go," James uttered, retreating before anything else developed.

That sure was a sorry mess of a conversation. They hadn't even discussed why James was here. He had forgotten to ask Samuel about that as it had turned into a rant-athon of sorts.

Never mind, I guess I shall play this my own way, James commented to himself. *Samuel isn't one that seems to be on the ball right now. He needs time to collect himself and regain some whimsy.*

11

Meanwhile, Astrid was very entertained as he witnessed a super angry James storming out of Samuel's grand establishment.

Awww, the golden boy isn't so golden anymore. What a terrible shame, I must say. Astrid said to himself sullenly in thought.

This game of one-upmanship was taking a very disturbing turn but even more sinister was that Astrid didn't seem to be bothered by it in the least amount. Sneering as James got closer, marching right up to Isra as she marveled over her newfound horned friend, courtesy of Astrid's magical skullduggery.

"Where did that come from?" James probed as he pointed flat out at the black unicorn.

The thing that was causing all the havoc had prevented James from asking Samuel what his game plan was. But instead, all of that had to be swept to the side as more important things emerged. Namely this black unicorn that had come out of nowhere.

"Oh, him? I have absolutely no inclination whatsoever, but isn't he a magnificent stallion of a soul?" Isra cooed, still stroking the beautiful beast.

It wasn't until she realized that James had such a stern stare upon his face that Isra noted that something was amiss with the tall man.

"You don't approve of magical creatures?" she pressed eagerly while refusing to take herself away from the bold creature that had beckoned her to such fiendish sights lay before her eyes.

"It's not that I don't have a liking for them. Black unicorns are forbidden from this peaceful land. It is causing a lot of commotion with the man upstairs," James explained.

"Oh, I see..."

Isra motioned slowly then trailed off as she felt confused by James's wording. She gave him a perplexed glance as if he was an alien or some kind of species she didn't recognize.

"Who is the man upstairs?" Isra asked as her eyes narrowed at James, carefully scrutinizing him as she wished to learn more about his cause. And as to why such a thing as a beautiful dark creature could cause such a ruckus. It was unfounded to her that it could be true, but apparently that was the way of it.

"Oh, there's no actual physical man. I meant it as more of just a figure of speech." James misled her. Well, he couldn't tell Isra the truth of who the gentleman in the building upstairs really was because no doubt that would lead to serious repercussions, which with recent events was actually best avoided. "Perhaps that is a conversation for another time."

James went back on himself, changing the subject swiftly. He didn't want Isra digging too much into areas that could be seen as dangerous territory so he had to sort of sway her off the path so to speak. Isra said nothing. She was still eyeballing James almost as though she was awaiting some sort of instruction from him as to what the next course of action was. Honestly, she wasn't sure why they were here in this strange land to begin with but being a witch she figured there was much more going on than what was being relayed to her.

Call it a suspicious mind or maybe it was just her intuition, but Isra was considering that a lot of stuff around her wasn't what it seems. And she wasn't wrong because the man responsible for creating that black beauty of a being was still lurking behind the bluebells watching her every move as she conversed with James.

Unbeknownst to Isra, Astrid was waiting for her and James to disappear so he could do his thing and talk to this dark entity he had summoned up out of nowhere, but they seemed to be taking their sweet time. James stalled Isra by changing the range of chatter so she didn't focus on the same topic she had instigated and also delayed their departure time. However, Astrid wasn't a patient man, so he figured it was best he made his own moves.

"I guess I will see you soon. Much sooner than either of us had in mind," Astrid muttered before he clicked his thumb and index finger together, dissipating in a puff of gray smoke before anyone could notice.

Astrid didn't waste any time in returning back to Shambre Fell, banking on the fact that Isra had hopefully decided to take residence there while also hoping James would not be present as he wanted some alone time with her for their next impromptu meeting. One where for the first time she would not see him in his raven form so it would be like she was meeting him all over again. Only he'd have precedence in rejoicing because Astrid could now be himself instead of hiding behind the light facade that had been concocted for him.

No more lies. No tomfoolery. This was the real deal.

Astrid was about to get knee-deep into some serious dark boundaries and most importantly he'd be pissing Samuel and James off and that was motivation in itself. Never mind that he was about to reunite a dark demoness with her long-lost daughter that also happened to be Isra's ex best friend, Everilda. Having a little rendezvous with Isra in order to facilitate that event was the least of Astrid's problems.

He carefully surveyed the robust green grass bank that surrounded Shambre Fell. It was saturated in a huge mass of it with only some shrubbery in the form of rose bushes and some beautifully ripe fruit trees being in it. The rest was all green. Then the magnum opus itself: a tall spindling gray tower spiking up into the sky in this secluded space in the middle of nowhere. It was designed specifically to be another world of which only someone really drawn to the magics would want to live here.

I mean, that was the idea behind Samuel's grand plan. He had to tempt the wicked side of Isra. The childlike side that lived by imagination and fantasy that saw things only in shades of wondrous colors of the rainbow. That was how Shambre Fell came together. A piece of Isra's youthful heart and Samuel's artistry blended perfectly with magic. How else would he have gotten her attention but to place some visual imagery in front of her face? It was classic psychology really, something that Samuel excelled at without question.

Astrid however didn't plan on telling any tall tales. He wanted to be up front with Isra and while he was going to have made the odd adjustment here and there for the most part he was going to be truthful with her. The small justification would be getting her around to his way of thinking but Astrid did really fancy a challenge.

"She must be around here somewhere. James wouldn't have taken her back to Spirisity after the fiasco with the unicorn, so it's either here or..." Astrid put his fingers to his lips after he said it, deep in thought. "...or Wingdom's!"

He quickly remembered the academy was still home to Isra for now unless she had taken her leave, permanently. Then Shambre Fell would be the next logical place for her to take up residence. Astrid fathomed since it was a fabricated realm created out of wonder and imagination it wouldn't be hard to get Isra to metaphysically occupy the humble abode. All she had to do was latch onto the door and turn the knob. How hard could it be?

The sun was rising. A beautiful mass of orange and yellow rays began coming into view. They were gently fluttering across the dusk skies. And then that was when Astrid caught sight of a tall woman hidden beneath a midnight blue velvet cloak lurking around in the grounds of this wondrous paradise. Icy white golden ringlets poking out of the cloak made Astrid take note as this was a sure indication that it had to be Isra.

Seizing his chance, as who he presumed to be Isra, stopped to admire the roses on the red and violet rose bush, Astrid made his approach. Striding along swiftly, he got closer and closer to her before his mysterious female could change her mind. Again, under the assumption this was indeed Isra. As Astrid got up close and in her face, he realized his assumption had been exactly right.

There she was. Those stunning emerald green eyes glinted back at him in fear and amazement, looking startled as those fiery green balls were all over him. It gave him a chuckle as he knew she could send a lightning bolt headed straight for him at any moment if she deemed the cause to be worthy enough. But Astrid wasn't some lovestruck pansy that would flee at the first sight of her unleashing her real self. Her darkened heart lay within her treacherous and tortured soul. He decided to take the lead in this awkward situation and he did that by warmly tapping her on the shoulder and announcing his existence in the way he knew best.

"Do not concern yourself, for there is nothing to fear. I am just a humble traveler in this terrain of bluster and blasphemy," he explained as Isra gave him a presumptuous look like she expected this kind of line.

Isra resisted the urge to turn away from him and dropped her arms by her sides, but maintained good focus with the rose bush because for some reason she felt comfortable having reasonable distance between her and this handsome beau who had landed in her midst.

"Aha, and do I look like some prissy girl primed for properness and formality?" she retorted in an icy tone.

"I am sorry. I didn't mean any offence," Astrid cut her off with his reply. He was a little confused that she was so hardened in tone. He'd expected better than this. Okay, maybe not a wide-open book, but maybe she'd have been somewhat receptive to him.

"Then don't address me as if I am some kind of regimental empress of the realm," she acknowledged coldly. Before she folded her arms, pressing them snugly across her chest, she emitted her primal fury as she stood facing him, wondering if he had the balls to take on her cold, flashing glare.

"All right," Astrid cajoled at her. "Let's skip the formalities, shall we? I'm Astrid. And you are Isra," he said quietly as Isra's wide green eyes practically fell to the floor, at least visually speaking as her head was still positioned onto her body. But she almost fainted at the shock of it as she tried in vain to gather her footing and her mental composure.

How could this stranger, this baffling yet handsome and well-endowed man know my name? Isra thought to herself, looking awfully puzzled at the seemingly very pleased Astrid. "And how do you happen to know my name?" she asked him in a methodical tone.

At least now he had Isra's full attention. That was better than her almost running away from him in terror, which to be frank, she could still do. She still stood close to the rose bush, a symbolic stance that told Astrid that she felt vulnerable and yet also that she was someone very precious. A rare article that could only be found in the most arcane of domiciles.

"There is much to know, of which I would like to divulge to you in person but first we must slip away from here. Eyes and ears will be all over us in these parts. It is safer for both of us if we go somewhere more familiar," he hinted to her with a sweet smile as if he gently priming her, getting her to go along with his reasoning but treading very lightly so as to not upset her delicate vivacity.

Isra kept her arms folded in a defensive manner as she continued to glare at him but the stare now slightly less frozen as Astrid seemed to have brought some warmth inside her. Out of the blue, she now looked merely confused rather than fearful or wanting to castrate him. And Astrid considered this progress. He liked his manly parts and would have hated to lose them, even if they were artificial for his beautifully constructed human form.

"What gives you the impression I will come away with you, dear heart?" Isra needled him, giving him the third degree.

Most would be perturbed by her cold, icy stares and her rigid stance in which she refused to budge an inch. She wouldn't give him any kind of lee way whatsoever, but Astrid was unaffected.

"You'll come along, and I won't have to drag you by your precious golden hair, girl. For you will come of your own accord," he mused confidently, leading to another bemused stare from Isra.

"And what makes you so sure of that claim to give yourself so much credit for something you are lacking the know-how in?" Isra prodded sternly.

She wasn't just giving him a good old interrogation. She was taking everything he said and dissecting it piece by piece. Questioning everything that came out of his mouth and analyzing the hell out of it until she was certain he was to be trusted. Or at least somewhat at any rate.

"Well, it isn't my endearing charm, sweetie, but I know a thing or two about inquisitive females. You won't be able to resist my wiles," Astrid chortled, laughing as he said it which was also very baffling to Isra.

It was strange having a man tell her what to do. A man detailing to her exactly how something was going to go and her not protesting in any way. But yet she found herself not wanting to rip his head off and staple it to a wall, like most males who had unfortunately crossed her path, wronging her with their unsightly behavior. Not that she'd kill them or something as drastic as that, but men hadn't been Isra's strong point since that hapless soul, Jonathan. She found them oh so piteous and useless to her now. It was unlikely she'd take up with a man again but now having such a strong-willed fellow talk to her in this manner and she was pretty much going along with it. Well, it was bewildering to say the least.

Once again, Isra found herself in unfamiliar terrain, on shaky ground where she wasn't sure if she was supported by the universe or whether she was about to plunge knee deep into melancholy. *That's odd. I am normally so sure of what I want. If a man gets on my sails I just deal with him and move on but this one has got under my skin. I cannot pinpoint what it is about him that has me so entranced,* Isra voiced quietly to herself in thought.

Astrid felt bold as Isra flashed him a cold stare. It gave him confidence and a sense of power. Like something was surging inside his well-kept body really amping up the masculinity in him. That made him feel like he was the one in control here.

Having only met this stranger a mere few moments ago it was so odd to Isra that she was allowing herself to converse with him when the old her would have just run a mile. However, there was something quite entrancing about him. Something that compelled her not to rip him to shreds for some bizarre reason she couldn't fathom, as well as a strange notion that she had met this individual, this charming Astrid fellow, somewhere before. But where they had crossed paths Isra had no idea of. And it was bugging the living shit out of her, because as he stared at her, his burning golden eyes all over her scanning every single part, Isra felt like Astrid knew something about her, a tasty tidbit of information that he was keeping concealed.

Oh yes, there was something very sneaky about this Astrid. Almost like he was a chameleon. One minute you could see him in his bright red coloring and then the next he'd gone and changed on you, causing you to work even harder to figure out just what the hell he was all about.

"Why do I not want to kill you?" Isra questioned with a slightly worried glance.

It concerned her because although she didn't have any desire to commit acts of violence, but it wasn't her usual approach when it came to bumptious men who thought they could order the woman around however they pleased.

"Now, now," Astrid coaxed. His tone was a tiny bit snide and Isra could detect the smallest hint of repulsive sarcasm but she chose to ignore this.

"Let's skip the pleasantries, shall we?!" Isra muttered with a half laugh. She wasn't impressed. "Normally I'd roast your kind alive. And feed them to the wolves. So why am I not doing that?" she asked again, feeling mortified now why she was drawn to this human, if that is what he was. It wasn't exactly easy for her to dissect this one apart and analyze his every move. She wasn't going to roast a man alive or feed him to any kind of beast, but saying that made her feel as though she still maintained some control over men.

"I know you, Isra," he whispered, lifting her chin up with his free hand so he could look deep into her bewildering emerald green eyes. "I know you've had a lot to deal with in your young life. You've had to grow up quickly in your short but eventful tenure, having your heart broken and discarded as if it was something meaningless. And now you have this whole bittersweet tang about you to guard just how hurt you really are. And yes, you gave your heart up to Hell and thought it would shield you by using this darkness as a protective layer but the truth is even with all that, you are still that vulnerable girl inside!"

He spoke carefully but with warmth. Astrid wanted to show that he cared for her and to show a sympathetic side to Isra, but being very smart as to not give pity because he knew she didn't want that. She had this whole badass thing going for her. She didn't want to be viewed as weak or some wretched soul that reigned in misery. Isra was stronger than that.

Astrid stopped as he realized Isra was not responding to him. Either she was mad, shocked, or just plain bemused as to how he knew all about her background. Literally he had spouted out nearly every detail that had made her who she was today. Anyone else would have taken the initiative to either smack the truth out of Astrid or they'd have grilled him on how he happened to know all that but Isra was mute.

He paused before he confessed meekly, "I've been following you for a very long time. Both me and Samuel have had many awkward and somewhat violent discussions pertaining to you, although it's not as bad as it sounds. He just can't handle the idea of me being close to you."

Astrid couldn't help but snigger at that last part. Samuel really had tried all he could to get Astrid to stay away from Isra. It was ironic and yet also comical that nothing Samuel had mustered had got Astrid to shift his focus away from her. The light bringer had lost the battle on this one. He tried to stifle the amusement as he carefully examined Isra's reaction to his mind-blowing disclosure he had unleashed from his mouth onto her person in such a forward and fearless manner.

"You've been *following* me?" the witch asked him with a sniping glare.

She wanted to peel herself away from this dark-haired fellow as fast as she could, but for some reason, she couldn't. There was a magnifying attraction keeping her pressed in her solid stance. Just one movement would allow her to be forced onto his firm yet slender body, forcing her to stare at the silvery slithers of gray in his unkempt hair.

"For a very long time. Months at least. But it has felt like hundreds of years," he assured her quietly.

"How very stealthy of you. You are a very bold and brash man, Astrid. Coming to find me when I am such a villainous and evil creature. Do tell me, where did you find such balls? I'd love to toy with them." Isra laughed although Astrid couldn't tell if she was being serious.

Astrid imagined he wouldn't find much humor if she was being literal in her wording, but he found that like many things about Isra, he was only just beginning to unravel the mystery of her. For now, he would put this disturbing thought aside hoping it was just her dark facade shouting very loudly to scare him off.

"It is true. I am still a stranger to you, but believe me; I know nearly everything there is to know about you. I've been by your side throughout," Astrid discharged, finally feeling free of the guilt as he unloaded the burden of spying on Isra for such a tenuous time. He was now finally able to be himself around her. "I've never had anyone who has been in my life in that attentive and yet generous manner."

Isra breathed out in a low voice. She was shocked to learn that someone was so close to her but she had no inclination of it or who they were. It was baffling to her that someone would bother to take the time over her. "Perhaps I may accept your compelling yet wonderfully insightful proposal to go along with you, but may I request something?"

Isra spoke with a soft yet concerning look on her face. She seemed to be preoccupied with something. Maybe even worried but her eyes weren't saying much so nothing could be divulged from this alone.

"Of course, anything for you, Trouble!" He'd retorted in a sardonic yet affectionate manner, giving her a sweet pet name which only displayed his deep sated attraction to her because he was so free to show Isra how he felt about her.

Isra looked slightly perturbed at this remark but for some reason she felt comfortable in his presence and that was a bizarre emotion for her to feel. This man, although Isra knew men to be callous creatures filled with deceit and splendid weaponry designed to tear a heart, appeared very much genuine. Perhaps he really and truly did have her best interests at heart. It was ironic that she had barely known him but yet felt so alive staring into those golden yellow eyes of his. The very same eyes that had been laid upon her robust form ever since he had first caught sight of her.

For some bewildering reasoning beyond her comprehension, Isra felt compelled to go along with whatever this entrancing gentleman said. And although a quaint rendezvous wasn't in her plans, she figured it would help to pass the time while she did her utmost to figure him out.

"So, are you going to be occupying this modest yet characteristic château?" Astrid asked with eager interest.

He was trying to locate her whereabouts exactly because knowing her dwelling would be a lot easier than using his senses to sniff her out since stalking her was one of his most frequent passions he'd have found that much more simple if he knew where to find her at all times. As crazy and creepy as it sounded, Astrid felt like he could keep watch over her better in this way.

Isra hesitated to answer him, staring back and forth at the tall spindling tower that dominated Shambre Fell wondering what it would be like to be in such a place like that. She considered the idea but still wasn't quite understanding how this fitted together. *How could one live somewhere just by the ideal home turning up out of nowhere?* Isra thought to herself as she paused again, keeping the moment lingering between her and Astrid.

He stood there awaiting her response, clearly keen on whatever she had to say. Standing gallantly in front of her as if he might stop her at any second if she tried to take her leave.

I still don't know this man and yet he stares at me in such a manner that he presumes to know me very well. Almost like we are long found acquaintances or so he believes, anyhow. But what does he want with me? Isra murmured in thought as she pursued the idea that her and this strange Astrid fellow may indeed have a connection.

Although such a thing would be preposterous to Isra. It would have required her to believe in love and all that namby pamby stuff that went along with it and frankly Isra had no time for that crap.

"I have not made a decision on that yet," Isra countered to him with a sullen glance. She gave the illusion as if there was hatred billowing up inside her which was ever so not causally directed at this bewildering male of whom was asking her so many questions.

"Ah, well, it's no pickle, firecracker. I am sure you will come to some kind of arrangement. It really is an iconic edifice. It would be a real shame to see it go to waste. So cruelly abandoned like this," Astrid mouthed quietly.

He had his index finger and forefinger placed across his lips thoughtfully as if to hint to Isra that she should just go ahead and take residence in Shambre Fell. Isra seemed puzzled again but this time she had a glint in her eye as if she was suspicious of something. The way her eyes flashed at Astrid giving him a full view of their lime green glow gave him the impression she wasn't as dumb as she made herself out to be at times. Maybe it was just another cover up to hide who she really is deep within. Astrid conferred in thought.

It was funny for Astrid, but he said nothing. He simply eyeballed Isra carefully, waiting for her marvelous reply that would no doubt inspire yet more delectable conversation between them.

"There's something peculiar about this habitation," Isra began before she too put her fingers to her lips inquisitively before looking upwards at the grand gray tower that was casting a dark shadow across the land. "It's been desolate for years, maybe even centuries, and yet I could not find a single speck of dust. Don't you find that mystifying?" she said to him in a low voice, only mirroring his same tone with her.

"No, I don't. Should I find it strange?" Astrid asked with a small half smile.

It was a flirtatious yet friendly gesture that showed his prominent yellow golden eyes as he was almost caught blushing, having so much joy radiating over him with something so simple as a beaming grin. One that surely could only be complimented with a kind smile from our lovely lady witch in return no doubt. Astrid would have appreciated that very much, of course. But small barely-made efforts were good enough for him for now just to show some interest, if nothing else.

These two souls that were barely anything more than strangers were matching up to each other and neither of them had any inclination of it. Even more outlandish was the fact that Astrid was preparing to take Isra under his wing and she was completely clueless as to what he had in mind. But of course, that was a deliberate act on his part. Astrid didn't believe in revealing one's strategy while being so close to the conclusion that was in sight as one tiny misdeed could send everything to hell. It was better to remain inscrutable rather than making one's intentions plain, and leaving everything to chance as you weren't clever enough to conceal your motives.

"I guess not," Isra concurred to him with a wistful look.

She looked to the beautiful morning skies lit up with rays of golden yellow and warm orange as if she expected them to give her some kind of message. It was silly of her to think things like this, but she believed there was more to a morning sunrise than just a simple blast of flashy golden light. No, there was something magical about the way the sun came rising up, taking the place of the moon as day dawned in. Something wonderfully mesmerizing that made her eyes surge with joy as she felt the heat from the majestic sun on the back of her skin. There was nothing like it. Nothing in the world.

"So, shall we go then?" Astrid called to Isra, swiftly knocking her out of her translucent daydream. Clearly, he had noticed she was off elsewhere in a bubble, completely cut off from all civilization in a world of her own thoughts.

"Err, yes..." Isra trailed off.

Shaking off some dust from her dress, she felt the sun move away from her again. She was somewhat startled but also increasingly aware of what was around her. It was almost as if Isra had x-ray vision as she looked into Astrid's eyes, seeing this cold, lonely man standing there in her midst. Even with his tired, shimmery golden eyes and mass of silvery gray hair, there was something inexplicable about him. Something that Isra couldn't fathom.

But as she tried to turn away from him, she felt a fiery bolt of invisible energy hit her; it was powerful enough for her heart to feel it. So although she could not view it with her own eyes, it was intense enough as it left a twinge of pain in her upper chest, just above her heart, which stopped as soon as she resumed her focus on him again.

"All right; no time like the present, girl!"

Astrid signaled to her with a sweetness in his voice but yet he was also being forceful. Not quite commanding as such, but still exhibiting his predominance over her which was markedly shown as he waved his finger at her signaling for her to come forward. Astrid suddenly changed his tone, putting his finger to his lips again in a thoughtful position as he realized that there could be a better way of going about things. So, taking the conversation to his way of thinking, Astrid piped up.

"Say, how do you fancy meeting me in the clearing at sunset? It's not that far away from here. I hear it's spectacular to sit there and watch the melancholic beaming entity meet its temporary death."

"Sounds most intriguing," Isra replied in a rather lacking tone.

Maybe she didn't appreciate Astrid's remark about the sun, but it was hard to tell what was on her mind since she didn't give a single shred of a clue with her sullen looks and fleeting glances. I guess that would be a very clever tactic supposing one was dealing with a mortal enemy or someone who could potentially rip you in half. Perhaps in Isra's mind it was better to be well armed by not giving away too much of who you are but Astrid already had the upper hand on her there.

"Great, then we shall cross paths here again just before the sun goes down. But remember, it's just in that clearing between the trees. You can't miss it. More importantly, you won't miss me either as I'll be standing ready to greet you," he announced happily with expectation.

It might have seemed way too presumptuous, but Astrid reached over for Isra's hand at once, taking due care to touch the soft skin that she so delicately possessed and he couldn't help himself. His fingers found themselves stroking her skin in a rhythmic manner as he gently lifted Isra's hand with his own free hand and brought it up to his warm moist lips.

Without hesitation and also ensuring that she didn't have the chance or time to run away, Astrid gave Isra a warm smile before proceeding to kiss her hand. His lips sank down onto her soft buttermilk skin as he caressed her gently before lifting his lips away. Astrid brought his eyes forward as he reached Isra's face to see her perplexed reaction. However, he noted she wasn't in any way scared but all she gave him was a dazed look with some slight pinkness that came with her blushing at his actions. Astrid's charming gesture had thrown Isra as he had expected but he felt gratified to do it.

The conversation was awkward as Isra stumbled over her reply to him. "I am sure I will do my best not to let it slip. Sunset then."

She backed away a little after answering him, almost ready to turn on her heels and about to spin off in the opposite direction as fast as her little legs would carry her but Astrid changed the tact just in time much to her bemusement.

"Yes, sunset. It was a pleasure to finally meet you, Isra." Astrid breathed in her direction. He also struggled to find words but he settled on the final one that rang true in his ears. "It was an honor."

This time he did not make a grand gesture of touching her or smiling. Astrid stood there taking all of her magnificence in, almost becoming disoriented within himself as he fixated on nothing but Isra. Isra only looked at him, giving him a confused glance in return. She didn't really know how to react in this deeply intimate situation that she was experiencing. And with a male, no less! But she was going with her gut instincts and since this Astrid fellow seemed friendly enough and his proposal intrigued her. Isra had decided against her normal choice of judgment to take a chance on him, and whatever tasty salivating morsel of knowledge he would be revealing to her in due course. For his intention as he had made known was to converse with her, but somewhere private. Hence, their impending tryst they had arranged for later on this evening.

Of course, Isra normally would have questioned such insanity over a thousand times. It really wasn't like her to just swan off with a transient being like this. And not having one single scrap of knowing of who the hell he was because she only had what he had disclosed to her to go on. So Isra followed Astrid freely in a blind daze, clearly uninformed of his agenda and just what he had in store for her.

Of course, it wasn't going to be dangerous for Isra to be in such close proximity with Astrid. He had no intent to harm her and wouldn't dream of such a gruesome feat; he just wanted to be close with her, even if this was the only chance he had of doing just that. Astrid was gently taking Isra along with him and making it absolutely ambiguous that he was the one running the show. For once, dear Isra who found it normal to have someone else take the lead. Yes, she was having to forgo being the one in charge because this newfound stranger who claimed to be much more than just that was in complete subordination and all Isra could do was sit back and enjoy the ride because there was sure to be more to come.

And with Astrid dragging her along to goodness knows what in prime supervision of his plans, who knows what he had in mind for the sweet and chaste Isra.

12

James wandered alone in the woods, having left Samuel to wallow in his drunken misery so to speak, as the light bringer had been overindulging in his favorite tipple, that damned old Irish whiskey. Naturally, James was a spiritual soul at heart and the only place he felt truly at home was in nature's grand pasture. So, he had decided to take a stroll through the barren trees, hoping some tidbits of wisdom might come to him as he walked.

It's a nice enough day with sunset almost beckoning. Perhaps I'll find some inspiration. Maybe it's tucked away in the treetops and just waiting to stumble onto my head, or any other body parts there in that would lead to thoughts being made, and then I could come to some successful conclusion and perhaps also find peace. Yes, that is a nice thought indeed, James chorused to himself inside his head. He found being in the fresh air was already helping to alleviate some of the dramatic chaos that was in his wake.

James quietly strolled along at a reasonable pace when he suddenly caught sight of something he really didn't like the look of. But what was it? Whatever it was it had James's raw umber eyes practically standing at attention as he could only stand back and watch the gray-haired fellow in front of him.

A most elegantly dressed man for his barely-over thirty years was adorned in a delicately tailored white shirt and black linen suit trousers with a matching long gentlemen's jacket to match the entire ensemble. And the most interesting part of this man's features? Golden yellow eyes the same shade as the sun and they looked meticulously beady. In fact, they looked far too beady for James's liking.

"No, it can't be! Surely not. It's impossible..." James guffawed as he muttered to himself, jumping off into a tangent. "But how would he even muster such a thing? He has no magical abilities to speak of, or maybe he's truly a dark horse that we didn't know of. Oh, this is just fucking stupid!" James stammered and exclaimed angrily.

He marched up right in front of the gray-haired onlooker who looked incredibly bemused and quite entertained at the sight of James stomping around, thinking him to look quite like a terrifying child that had not been allowed to have some delightful play toy as he glared at the gray haired man with absolute bloody fury. Now within an inch of the increasingly amused onlooker, James stared right at him. His jaw dropped. James was completely speechless as he was now face to face with the man in front of him. It was made clear that the identity of this individual was none other than Astrid.

Somehow, he wasn't a raven anymore, but how such a feat could be achieved by a bird of Astrid's caliber was implausible to James. Unthinkable, even. How had he transformed into a fine magnificent creature that could only be described as masculine yet bold? Gone were the black feathers, replaced with a mass of hair that was more gray in color covering the top of his humanized head, only to contrast with those yellow golden beady eyes of his. How ironic, even as a human, he still had a mighty fine pair of eyeballs. Specifically useful for when he wanted to catch a glimpse of a certain female in the wee late hours, no doubt.

"How did you get like that? A human? No, it's preposterous. There is no possible way!" James stammered with a huff, still shocked beyond comprehension that Astrid had managed to pull this off. *It's unbelievable how he got like this! To be in such a form that he'd be able to have his wicked way with Isra and probably a lot more besides that. Actually, that last thought doesn't bear thinking about because no doubt with his benign obsession, that's the number one thing on his mind,* James chortled to himself in thought. He considered the situation just as Astrid was about to answer him.

"I have friends in high places," Astrid joked, giving James the biggest beaming grin he could possibly muster.

Oh, he loved this, not even caring that he'd been found out. Or maybe he wanted to get caught. The way he stood there, just so cocky and rigorous about it all suggested he really didn't give a shit.

"Right, and you are just out here loitering for the hell of it, I suppose?" James probed in a countering tone, evidently not believing Astrid or anything he was about to come out with.

"Yes, actually. Have you seen this?" Astrid pointed at the glorious mess of pink, orange, and yellow that dominated the usually cloudy skies. "It is beautiful."

Funny enough, Astrid had been with Isra for most of the morning and he hadn't even noticed that the sun was making its leave since he was so preoccupied with her making her appearance to him at any moment.

"A sunset! Great, but I've seen them all. As have you. Now seriously, how the hell did you become human?" James pressed Astrid with a forewarning glance.

"Not telling. Sorry if it bugs you. Actually, I'm really not that sorry," Astrid mocked, again his attitude was very sardonic and cheeky in nature. The man clearly thought he'd had this in the bag, knowing that the worst James could do was threaten him with running off to Samuel and spilling his dirty laundry to the light bringer without hesitation.

"Fine! But what are you doing down here? For real now. I want an answer," James retorted angrily.

He thought Astrid the raven could play humorously childish games but Astrid the human was giving him a run for his money. He was bold and brash and really didn't give a crap who knew. The balls of this man alone spoke volumes of who he was really about. Those forcefully glaring yellow eyes of his were all over James.

"What are *you* doing here?" Astrid asked, changing the subject.

He assumed by switching the blame onto James in a sense, he'd turn the tables without having to acknowledge his real reasoning in the first instance. Of course, Astrid had said he was looking at the sunset but when you consider he'd seen a million of them already, that wasn't exactly convincing. Again, the gray haired fellow was being manipulative; smiling as those lips of his smacked together so loud that you could hear the glee as his lips touched. He was obviously very entertained by this little showdown of which he didn't feel at all threatened by James because the way Astrid saw it, the only way was up from here.

"That is not for your knowledge. However, we aren't talking about me here. We are pertaining to you. As per fucking usual," James snapped back.

Astrid chuckled, feeling very smug as he chided, "So if I'm not telling you what I am doing and you refuse to tell me why you are here, we are in quite the predicament aren't we? Tell you what, why don't you piss off and I'll carry on enjoying the bounties of nature." Astrid mocked James with a snide grin, almost as though he was trying to taunt James but both sides were equally balanced here.

"No. I will not," James countered. Again, he was getting irritated by Astrid's superior attitude, like he was so untouchable. *It wouldn't take much to wipe that smug look off his face,* James pondered to himself. *All I have to do is mention one snippet of this to Samuel and this bad ass will be in more hot water than he can stand!*

"You should go," Astrid recited before pausing as he turned to the row of trees behind them. His eyes focused on a certain hawthorn of which next to it was a thicket. The very same that Isra would be emerging from any moment from now. "Isra is due to arrive here any second. If she sees you and me together, she's going to have questions. And if you keep annoying me, I might be all too inclined to fill in the blanks." Astrid had made his announcement with another snide and amused grin splashed upon his face. He practically glowed with how much power he wielded with that statement alone.

James was seething now. Almost spitting with rage. *This spewing of revelations was just getting better and much more forthcoming,* he cursed to himself in thought. "And what the devil are you doing interacting with her when you've been told damn knows how many times not to?" James questioned, folding his arms across his chest. Oh, he was getting pissed with Astrid's nonchalance. That was obvious now.

"Hmmm, not sure that's any of your business. I thought we'd set up a quiet little rendezvous in the forest. Picnic on the grass. Flask of steaming hot coffee. Cherry bake-wells wrapped in their dynamic gold foil so they don't spoil. All the treasures that immortal bliss has to offer, really," Astrid voiced with a sarcastic mannerism. "Of course, you aren't invited. So sod off," Astrid added with a hilarious glare.

James relented. "Fine. I'll go."

There was an echo of silence between the two males as though one didn't know just what the other was going to do and so the intensity lingered as though it were a toxic substance. Both men were very riled and also at war with each other verbally, both having thought they had the upper hand.

"I am interested to see how long it will be before another one of your messes lands you headfirst into more serious terrain," James mused before turning away.

James made haste to be cryptic now, not letting Astrid know just what he was thinking. It was all a game, you see. Astrid was used to having his own way and bullying those around him into giving in but James was a different brand of boldness Astrid wasn't used to. The truth was that James was a very similar personality to Astrid and so it was inevitable that they clashed. But James wasn't as vulgar as Astrid. He possessed some morals which probably irritated Astrid even more.

James was the think-then-do-it kind of type, and James was methodical. He'd look at a situation with a more compassionate view and think of the best resolution that would generate peace rather than trying to win some battle in which he would come out smelling of roses, whereas Astrid was all about being victorious and gloating at his enemies when he won the prize. However, James saw through Astrid's bullshit much easier than most. It was annoying to James that he still had to glaze over Astrid's infatuation with Isra and most likely some part of himself that he wasn't quite at peace with. But it was all showmanship.

Astrid was playing the role of the big, hard man and yes, it worked very well for him; but James wasn't really someone he could manipulate and that was probably why Astrid didn't take much of a liking to him. It was easier for the raven man to take jabs at James because let's face it; he had met his match in James. And in more ways than one.

"Whatever," Astrid scoffed at James, only this time his frown was menacing in nature as he huffed, "So what are you still doing here anyway? I thought you were pissing off."

"I am!" James retorted angrily, spinning around to face Astrid eagerly.

Both men were knee-deep embroiled in a verbal affray now and it was only a matter of time before one of them said something they would definitely not regret later.

"Good. Skedaddle then. Bye," Astrid mocked, waving to James as if he was signaling for him to depart without delay.

James threw a closed fist at Astrid as though he was about to knock Astrid down to the ground with just one punch. Unlucky, because Astrid was sharp in sight and saw it coming from a mile off, much to James's shock as he was a skilled swordsman with a whole host of other talents to boot.

"Aww, a boisterous one, huh? Don't even try it, boy," Astrid mouthed. The venom practically leaked from his lips as he said it.

As one would expect, Astrid didn't waste any time in dealing with James's attempted move to knock him dead onto the floor. Although not literally dead, of course. Astrid, with his robust physique, swiftly maneuvered himself, turning around to grab James from behind and then when he had a firm grasp on James's fist and arm, Astrid clasped James's fist in his own manly hands before twisting it behind James's back, leaving the hold in place for a couple of seconds as Astrid completely disarmed his rival.

To finish it off, Astrid flashed James yet another triumphant smile as he discharged his splendid move, releasing James from his tight grip. This left James reeling as he backed away a few spaces, nursing his sore fist and looking increasingly annoyed at Astrid of whom was still maintaining his solid stance, looking amazingly pleased with himself since he had shown James not to mess with him in any way.

Perhaps next time he will save his energy, Astrid murmured to himself in thought.

James swept some dust off his shirt and trousers, wiping it away in a brisk movement with his pain-free hand before facing Astrid again to deliver another confrontational remark, but this time James was going for a different tactic. Yes, he had been beaten, but there was still one way to wipe the smug look off Astrid's face and that was by doing the thing he should have done from the beginning of this whole debacle.

"All right, I'll let you have this one glorious victory," James smirked. "But after this, the next thing you do will be told, and believe me, it won't have to be something that's even remotely bad. But you best give credence that the second you slip up and execute anything that even smells distinctly iffy, I'm running all the way to Samuel before you can fucking blink!"

James scoffed before turning away. He was about to undertake his exit as he'd had his excitement in the way of a fiery confrontation and after that the whole idea about finding inspiration on a charming nature walk had long dissipated from his mind. James headed straight for the narrow golden path that would lead him out of the forest and into terrain more familiar to him, such as the bend the enjoined both Spirisity and Seclara. It was evident that James had endured enough of Astrid's flabbergasting conversation for one early evening and now it was time to retire.

In any event, Astrid wasn't satisfied with the showdown he'd had. He just had to take one last jab at James, just for the pure hell of it because he felt like it. Standing back and looking in James's direction,

Astrid bellowed at the top of his voice, "Oh, go ahead and run to Samuel. I dare you. Do it and stop blabbering already. Bring me back a souvenir from when he smashes up the place from the sheer frustration of you taking so long to relay my shenanigans to him." Astrid joked as he threw yet another threatening jibe in James' way, "Hey, I'm so good at this shit maybe I should be called the conductor of mischievous sneakery!"

"Whatever!" James shouted back in Astrid's direction.

And just as he was about to walk off into the distance, who did he see emerging from the trees? He was pretty sure as to who it was. Long flowing midnight blue velvet cloak. Golden white hair with ringlets poking out from the cloak's hood. Piercing lime green eyes that were almost shimmering with interest at what was going on.

Oh yes. It was none other than Isra. And she had walked smack bang into the middle of Astrid's and James' fiery culmination that had apparently unfolded in front of her eyes. Just imagine if she had been present there long enough to get wind of exactly what the two men were squabbling about. If Isra had learned the truth then the consequences that befell Astrid, James and even the light bringer Samuel did not bear thinking about.

13

Isra fully materialized out from beyond the trees with a puzzled look resting upon her face. Her eyes were narrowed and staring at both Astrid and James of whom had keen attentiveness toward her. Both parties were overly concerned as to exactly what she had witnessed and heard with her ears pertaining to their vile confrontation.

Isra gasped, putting a hand to her mouth in shock at what she had witnessed. "Oh my. I don't wish to intrude, but I feel like I may have stumbled upon something I shouldn't have here."

She didn't appear in any way vexed so maybe she hadn't heard anything particularly explosive. Perhaps she had just caught the tail end of it. But Astrid was taking no chances. He had to create an aberration and be swift on his heels before anything else could commence. Astrid stepped out in the way. A real nice diversion as he smugly blocked James from getting to Isra, quickly taking the lead as he motioned to her.

"Oh, worry not, Trouble. I just came across this peasant. He was wandering around in the woods and we got chatty about the wonders of life and such quaint antiquities. I'm sure he will be off on his merry way now," Astrid recited in James's direction that was made plain that it was a hint as Astrid glared at James with stern expectation.

"Yes, it's no quandary," James muttered quietly. "I was off on my travels anyhow. It was nice to have met you again, Isra." James smiled at her warmly before he returned Astrid's fierce glare with one of his own to match it, giving Astrid a taste of his own medicine of which the former raven could only silently growl under his breath before stone-facing James with another cold, icy stare.

James made one last look at Astrid and Isra before turning around and disappearing beyond the bend in amongst the trees, scarpering before any more heated exchange could be delivered.

THIS LONG-AWAITED departure was much to Astrid's glee who was pleased that James had finally made his exit. The only issue was that James was in a position to knock all of Astrid's plans right out of the window and potentially blow them to smithereens especially if Samuel got to it in time. But Astrid had a sneaking suspicion he was bluffing. You know, the art where one would say something just to get a reaction but wasn't fully prepared to go ahead with it. That was the guise that James gave off to Astrid, so he tossed it away like it was a dull ache foreboding in the back of his skull.

Astrid wasn't at all worried about that. However, the thing that Astrid was having issues over was Isra. He needed to attain close receptivity from her by getting her to trust him, taking it slow with baby steps because he knew that trust was a huge factor for her and if he wasn't careful she'd misjudge him as every other treacherous soul she had ever laid eyes on. He would earn her trust by gently engaging her to interact with him and learning all about her thought processes. You know, what made her think these thoughts about the human world in general and what caused her to doubt that people could ever be good as far as she was concerned. Astrid was willing to risk it all in order to attain ultimate intimacy with Isra and not the sexual kind.

He knew it was important for him and Isra to have a meeting of minds and then he could finally claim her as his, even if his plan was to totally explore the dark side of her. And perhaps also exploited a little just to tick Samuel off; which Astrid had to admit was going to be rather enjoyable since he had totally shifted away from the whole mission against darkness thing.

But that wasn't important right now. He had Isra right here in his grasp, physically present for him to do whatever he wanted with her, on a non-sexual tangent of course, because he was sure she was still a virgin. But all good things come to those who wait. For if it turned out Isra was still pure in body, he would ensure that she was treated with respect when that glorious moment arrived.

Astrid was about to strike up a bit of banter when Isra interrupted his thoughts all of a sudden with her broad asking, "So how do you know the tall man James that was here just now? I know you attempted to make out you had no knowledge of him, but your body language spoke very differently."

Uh oh, maybe she did hear more than she let on. Oops. Perhaps I should have studied the situation better before James stormed off. I should have analyzed Isra and him and worked out exactly what kind of problems would arise before she got incredulous about it, Astrid mused to himself in thought. *Then maybe any misconceptions could be nipped in the bud before anything got out of hand. If Isra did have any ideas of what might be occurring myself and James, I could snap them in half before that boy could shoot daggers at me. Maybe she could be swung around to my perspective and then we'd have no limitations minus the ones she chooses to create. And thus, for myself as well, but at least then we'd have some kind of idea of what is standing between us here,* Astrid summarized to himself as he turned back to Isra.

She was awaiting an answer from him and he'd have to be snappy if he was going to give her the right one. Clearly the girl was curious and Astrid just dragging this out was only going to fuel her need for snooping into the intricate weave that was so obviously dangling between Astrid and James. Two foes, very much at each other's throats. Extremely heated and both yearning to take the other out whether it was out of childish pranks or a more serious issue altogether. It was self-explanatory that there was no love lost between the two, even if they did act almost polite at times.

"Actually, I don't really know him that well," Astrid stated precisely as though any other interpretation would deeply offend him. It was as though if someone was even brave enough in making the slight connection that there was more between him and James other than contempt for one another that Astrid would get super irked by it.

"Oh. I apologize for my overestimation then. I just assumed by the way you two souls were looking at each other like a pair of hungry wolves that there was something between you. Other than resentment, that is." Isra pronounced eagerly, clearly not worried about angering Astrid or overstepping her mark.

But as Isra was someone that called it as she saw it, that small detail such as tactfulness really didn't factor into her thought process. It was a case of saying it and dealing with it. She wouldn't lose any sleep if you were offended. As far as she was concerned, you'd better get over it and yourself quick as lightning or better yet, don't ask for her opinion. Life was far too short to consider why you might hurt somebody's delicate whiney feelings as far as Isra saw it. So no bother.

This Astrid fellow is a big boy. He's had far more intrusive questions aimed in his way than this. He can take it from me. He's practically dragged me down here in the middle of nowhere anyhow and honestly what was that for? Just for us to sit down and talk? Please, I know he has an agenda here. I like the fact he's intrigued by me. I am a radiant eccentric of sorts so it flatters me that someone would want to be in my company, but come on; he hasn't done it for shits and giggles now, has he? Or maybe I'm some dumb blonde that's stupid enough to fall for anything, but honestly, I feel he has more in mind then he lays claim to, Isra pursued in her thoughts.

"All right," Astrid relented. "The annoying, tall, mousy-haired man has riled me a few times but it's nothing to worry your pretty little head about, Trouble. I can handle him. I've dealt with worse," Astrid concluded in a cryptic voice clearly illustrating that he was ready for whatever James said pertaining to him or to him. It really didn't make a difference to the brash Astrid, for he was made of stronger stuff than most.

"Aha. I knew there was something between you!" Isra scoffed wickedly as though she got off on being right, like there was a sadistic part of her that enjoyed seeing Astrid admit that James got on his wick. Perhaps there was more to Isra than she was letting on, but since she was being so coy and refined, there would be no way of telling what she was really thinking.

"There is something between James and I, but I can guarantee you, sweetheart, it ain't nothing good. Come. Sit," Astrid murmured as he seated himself on the green grass getting a clear view of the sunset that was lighting up the dusk evening remarkably.

Astrid only took a moment before he gently patted on the grassy bank that was guarded by the dynamic pathway of. It was then that he could be seen carrying a huge wicker basket that he had tightly positioned under his arm. He'd had it with him this whole time and Isra hadn't even noticed.

"I guess that would be pleasant," Isra muttered as she plopped herself down onto the grass. She smoothed out the pleats from her black and purple lace dress as she sat cross legged on the ground next to Astrid, although she was a few more inches away from him then he'd have liked, but that was okay. He'd have her closer to him soon enough.

"I don't bite," he joked in Isra's direction.

You'd think she'd have thought out her wonderfully bizarre defense mechanism but instead her jaw dropped, leaving her mouth wide open. Isra obviously had no inclination of what to say. The shock of Astrid's blunt and yet also forward comment was written all over her face.

"Bite?" Isra questioned him meekly. "Nobody said anything about biting."

She didn't say anything else. It was as though if she opened her mouth she wouldn't know what to say to him. Isra wasn't used to having a man command her in such a way that he practically demanded her to be at his will.

Astrid was just a lonely, kindhearted stranger but yet he was so much more. Those foreboding eyes of his darted around the place and at Isra swiftly in a nanosecond to catch even the slightest error made in his name. And then there was that coarse yet deep voice that emanated his masculinity, showing he had a physical prowess to him. One that showed Astrid was not only desirable but that he was also worth the wait even if someone had to wait a long time for him to place those strong hands on them. Just the thought sent tingles down Isra's spine. It was enchanting just being in his presence and having him watch her with his eyes and know every segment of what she was thinking in the same breath.

Astrid excused himself, giggling a little as he shrugged off Isra's fear in a heartbeat. "I meant I won't hurt you. Come closer to me. What's the worst that can happen if our knees touch? You won't catch anything from me, I promise, apart from the odd vile innuendo and sarcastic remark." Astrid chuckled to Isra with a wink.

He was hinting that she was safe to come nearer to him, but he'd be gentle with her. And in doing so, he decided to give her the answer she was seeking. Astrid didn't want this annoying bothersome area of interest to haunt their entire evening. No, it was best to sweep it up now and get it out of the way. At least metaphorically speaking anyway, because Astrid couldn't just sweep James up into a box with a broom and then slap him with it.

If only wishes were horses, he jibed to himself with a smug grin in thought. "As for James, he's just some peasant. Anyway, let's forget him. I brought you here to talk, though maybe we could admire the view," Astrid proposed as he pointed at the golden orange sun that was slowly diminishing from the sky as it got lower and lower as the minutes passed.

"Oh, that is just scrumptious," Isra recited with warmth in her heart.

A small smile appeared on her face as she watched the gold ball of fiery light slowly tumble down into nothing. It was effervescent as it made its final voyage before completely vanishing from the sky and thus darkness was descending upon the world.

"That it was indeed," Astrid agreed with her as a smile gleamed from his person.

Happily engaged, Astrid nodded his head before shifting toward the elegant basket he had prepared before their meeting. Oh yes, Astrid had put considerable thought into this. He'd gone to a lot of effort in order to come up with a supreme platter fit for a princess. Although Isra was not royalty, he had wanted to impress her sincerely by offering small gifts of gratitude.

He reached into the wicker basket and pulled out a silver steel flask before retrieving one golden foil-wrapped round object. From the look of it and the sweet scent it gave off you'd guess that it was some kind of dessert-type of food. But as he slowly unpeeled the foil away from it a shiny white round cake was revealed that had a sweet yet tangy cherry plastered on top, almost symbolic as Astrid went off into a tantalizing chorus in his thoughts. A lusty man he was, and he couldn't help himself because he desired her so badly. He admired Isra in front of him before turning his attention to his thought plan that was so deliciously unfolding inside his head.

That cherry on top of the icing wouldn't taste as good as her cherry that lies underneath her garments, but alas, I cannot tell her that I think of such sensual wonderments now. Astrid turned his wandering eyes to Isra with a seductive glint in them and before she knew what was happening, Astrid had pried his two fingers between her soft lips before feeding the cakey treat into her mouth while whispering in her ear, "That cherry might just be riper than you."

Isra resisted hard, but Astrid had already rehearsed what to do if she had attempted this. He was not allowing her to get any kind of handle on herself by slipping away from his strong hold. *Oh no, you don't, love. I've got you good.* He chuckled to himself in amusement before returning his affixing gaze unto her.

"I don't ... I've never ... not with a man!" Isra exclaimed, almost terrified at such a suggestion. One that was clearly explicit in nature. Isra was sure she didn't know what this bold man had meant by saying his delectable cherry was riper than she was but she was sure that the context of it was most definitely carnal.

"I know. I can tell," Astrid recited back to her.

He smiled right at her for some reason that Isra couldn't comprehend. Isra couldn't figure out if the news of her virginity still being intact was amusing to this man or whether he was smiling because something about it gave him a glint of happiness. Somewhere deep under her fabricated illusion about romance Astrid could see right through her deception of not wanting to yearn for another. Perhaps he believed that the truth of it was much more different that Isra had originally maintained. But still she didn't give in, keeping her stiff demeanor fully pressed on in this circumstance.

"Oh, don't worry; when the time is right, you will know that giving yourself away to someone, a most beautiful and handsome fella who loves you for you I might add, will be the most wonderful, passionate experience you have ever known!" Astrid verbally demonstrated as his finger drifted down to the folds of her dress. It hovered slightly above the sacred area of which Isra would be giving to another male.

Astrid so wanted to be that male. If he had any aspirations at all, this would be somewhere near the top. To be her first. For he was fond of her and it had been a very long time since Astrid had been fond of anyone. Still getting used to having hands instead of talons and fingers that could stroke instead of claws that scratched and tore open flesh, Astrid was very much savoring his time just being able to feel Isra even if he couldn't get past her forbidden boundaries just yet.

"I have not foreseen such an exciting development in my young life," Isra countered, almost knocking Astrid's deep compliment to her away, but he didn't take offence to it for he knew she only believed what she already knew to be absolute.

"It will come." He breathed slowly, taking her in again. "You have forever."

As he and Isra were sat in the newly beckoned night, Astrid couldn't help but be intrigued and also at the same time bemused by her beauty and ravishing endowment that made Isra ever so more appealing to him, but he was taken aback when yet again she interrupted his seductive thoughts.

"I might have been inclined to think so way back when Jonathan and I were courting, but then Everilda got her pasty hands all over him and that put paid to any impending futuristic notion that I might have a chance at being impure," Isra blurted out in a gravelling tone, as if she was both angry and riled at the same time.

Immediately, Isra had caught Astrid unawares as he suddenly remembered his part in the whole Everilda situation, of which he had not yet disclosed to Isra. *But there was no time like the present so best to just come out with it. If she doesn't scamper off with a scowl on her face like she wants to roast me alive, then I'm onto a good footing,* Astrid mused to himself comically. "Ah, Everilda Daughtry," Astrid said to her at once.

Isra's head shook, and Astrid couldn't work out if it was out of hatred or sheer disappointment as for the first time ever, Astrid saw bright red glimmers in the pupils of Isra's eyes, signaling the dangerous terrain he was in just by discussing this with her. But it was okay, Astrid could handle it. He could diminish her vile foul tempered behavior and restrain her if necessary. He knew how to go about this better than most. It was just by knowing exactly what to say to cool her heated self down in a fraction of a second. Even if it was exacted by force.

"You know her?" Isra pressed eagerly. Her face was frozen as she awaited Astrid to deliver to her what she believed he would agree with wholeheartedly.

"Indeed, I do. Prize-worthy, highly esteemed daughter of one of the most powerful warlocks in the land. The grand lord himself. Damien Daughtry. And a good friend of mine," Astrid cajoled in a stern manner as if he knew what was coming from Isra next.

"How wonderfully rotten for your friend to have such a failure for a daughter. I can't say I agree that Evie is highly esteemed, but you think whatever prattle you want to." She mocked him with a snide grin.

"Now now, there will be none of that," Astrid scolded her in warning with his finger pointing at her. "I understand you have your quarrel with her, but Everilda Daughtry is off limits," Astrid cautioned her before turning to her softly and whispering, "There are much more interesting ways to deal with a soiled bad apple and a witch yourself being dark must know that. Revenge in itself is its own reward, but one must endeavor to taste it slowly otherwise the apple when taken will be bitter instead of divine." Astrid reeled the words off his tongue as if he was imparting some important piece of wisdom although it sounded diabolically vile.

It was very abhorrent the way he had worded it, almost compelling enough to send an indirect instruction to Isra, like he had expected her to do something to follow on with his cryptic aphorism. There was a sinister glint in the gray-haired man's eye signaling that Astrid might well be exerting to lead Isra down a very wrong and well-trodden path much further than she had intended to go.

14

Isra was wandering alone in her favorite place. The cliff peak that was located in the mysterious land of Glamvein although she didn't know that was the place just yet. All she knew was that this was the very place she'd given herself up to the soiled ways of life and since then it had become a fond location for her to visit from time to time when she needed a moment to collect herself.

Isra had left that lustful Astrid man back in Shambre Fell, or at least the clearing beyond it anyhow. He was entrancing to her for sure and there had been no fault of his own that she had left. Isra had just needed space to breathe and coming here to this grand stature of a mountain top was perfectly isolated enough for her to just exhale all her concerns. The handsome yet disheveled fellow had been testing her patience a little. After he had told her very sternly that Everilda was off limits and then suggested to her that there were other ways to get back at those who had wronged her, it was safe to say that Isra was puzzled over the whole conundrum.

Isra wondered what Astrid's game plan was. She was baffled over how he had just appeared when she had wanted to be alone, almost magically offering up something when she had barely anything to lay claim to apart from her own self-reliance. It was almost too good to be true, but Isra had agreed to meet Astrid again, however that wouldn't be until dusk.

Since it was already past morning with the sun dancing around the dewy skies with shades of powder blue peeking out from behind the white fluffy clouds, Isra had plenty of time to kill until then, so sitting upon this cliff top would do for now. Just whiling away her cares, admiring the view that beckoned her eyes for it was luscious indeed. Masses of greenery in the form of hills and valleys that outshone for miles. Amongst it all was what seemed to be a quaint little village. Even from a distance, Isra could faintly make out what she perceived to be little modest townhouses. The poor and impeccably worse off types that resided in these picturesque little villages people lived in terrible conditions and small abodes that were just about considered sustainable to dwell in.

What a pretty atrocity it must be to be in such a place, Isra thought to herself quietly as a gray mass blocked her view.

Isra was immediately distracted by a shadow that appeared beside her, noting that this was the gray thing she had mistaken for something else. As Isra turned her head upward, she realized what the shadow was, noticing the red and blue coloring in the robust yet muscular body with bright amethystine purple wings to match it. Yes, it was indeed. It was Franco, the dragon Isra had created out of nowhere. Actually, she had forgotten all about him, so his materializing here was a surprise to her, but a happy one nevertheless.

Acknowledging the brightly colored creature fondly, Isra said calmly, "Oh Franco, dear boy. I had actually been careless and taken my leave from you but things have been testing me greatly."

She took care to explain herself with clear intention for she wanted him to understand that it wasn't a deliberate abandonment on her part. No, that wouldn't have been good for her to do but alas, Isra had been very busy. It was true she had been focused on other things, namely this Astrid fellow, James, the warrior type who had led her into the grand stature that was Shambre Fell, and the light bringer of whom she had met seconds after creating Franco. It was safe to say that Isra had a lot on her plate. She was absolute in her notion that it wasn't about to end any time soon. And likely neither would the confusion.

"I understand, dear heart," Franco commented with a wide-eyed glance. He was warm as his ruby red eyes glazed upon her in a transfixed manner as if he understood her predicament somewhat.

"Do you really? Because honestly, I am not sure if I do. For real, I've really been through it. I'm not trying to be one of those folk with a mentality for victim ship, but my goodness it just keeps coming. The confusion is the brunt of it, you see. The rest is merely just theater. Rehearsing for something much bigger," Isra confessed with a huge sigh.

The dragon had no judgment toward Isra, simply nodding as if he had experienced this sort of thing in times gone by. Franco, although barely anything more than the humble creation of a witch forged in darkness and power, had a basic summary of life despite his being very short thus far. It was as though the wild beast Franco was speaking from another dimension as he calmly voiced, "Well, life is designed to perplex us. The only challenging facet of it is whether we fall down at the waysides or if we rise high away from the morbid illusions into the translucent skies."

"You make it sound so easy!" Isra exclaimed with a slight laugh.

She felt like she was reading some old text from a volume that had been lost in the archives of time, probably lying there for centuries until someone awakened the magic that was to be found inside it. Franco spoke in such a wise tone and it was ironic since he had only been in existence for a few days, maybe less than that. Perhaps somehow in her revenge darkened subconscious she had manifested someone to guide her and show her the way on this hard, cold path she had entered into.

"It can be." Franco encouraged her with a warm smile even though it was hard to imagine through such large shiny white gold teeth sharpened to precision for the perfect kill.

"I can only hope with all my heart that you are right. It used to be a lot less of a puzzle. I knew exactly what I had to do. Now I have turned my heart away from all that is righteous and good. I have ridden myself of my betrayers including my former companion, Evie. And now I have this strange gentleman practically handing me friendship and loyalty plus trust and all that wonderful stuff that goes along with it, but he seems to be more than what he seems. Does that make sense to you? I am not sure it does to me," Isra mumbled although it seemed like a mild rant of sorts as she was muddled and unsure of herself.

"Nothing is what we perceive it to be. You can only go with the flow and find out where it leads with you when everything stops at once and that is only when you will have clarity. When you finally listen to the world around you," Franco expressed carefully before a loud rumble in his gut signaled he would have to depart soon. It was almost the same sound as a volcano only with no explosive chaos to go along with it.

Isra imagined that dragons needed to eat as much as any other creature so all she did was excuse him politely, "Well, thank you, friend. I expect you are ravenous. Your belly speaks loud and clear!" she mused with a giggle.

"Ah, my frank apologies, but a man has to eat," Franco murmured quietly.

"No problem at all, friend. I understand. I just came here for some quiet reflection. It's been a tiresome day and I am expected to meet Astrid again soon."

"Be well," Franco called to her as he launched into the skies disappearing again at a moment's notice.

It was then as the silence descended upon her that Isra recognized that something or someone was behind her. There was a pungent scent of vile breath lingering almost like rotten eggs or something equally grotesque. A dead animal, maybe. But whatever the foul smell was, it was horrid enough to make Isra unseat herself from the edge of the mountain peak only to find herself face to face with Everilda.

~

"WHAT IN GOD'S name are you doing here?" Isra screeched, absolutely furious to see her foe again after their last exchange of heated words. Isra scrunched her fist tightly only displaying how angry she was at Everilda.

"Relax. I'm not out to cause you any bother," Everilda exclaimed.

She looked weary, all done down in a gray dress that was fraying at the seams and stains of goodness knows what covering the delicate lace fabric that obviously needed a good cleansing in hot boiling water judging by the smell of her. It wasn't a pretty sight to behold; even Everilda's usually bright shimmering golden hair had lost its luster as it now barely went past her shoulders and with plenty of split ends to boot. So it wasn't just her clothing that was off.

"So what are you doing here?" came Isra's stern reply. Again, her arms were folded across her chest in a pressing manner as if she demanded answers instantly. And wasn't going to tolerate any funny business from Everilda. *I wonder why she reeks so badly of vermin. I guess being banished and expelled from the top gods of society really does lead to rock bottom. Perhaps it also means a lack of cleanliness too,* Isra joked in her thoughts. Yes, she clearly hadn't lost her sense of whimsy, for yet again she was making torrid fun out of Everilda's harsh predicament.

"I was just out for a stroll, happened to see you. Thought we might be able to talk. After everything in recent moons, I've really regretted the choices I made regarding you, me, and that sap Jonathan. And ... well, I feel awful about it," Everilda explained with a sigh.

It was odd to Isra because Everilda actually seemed genuine. There was a look about her that just spelled out that she was miserable deep inside. I mean, she was a wreck and not just in her physical appearance either. There was something off about her. It wasn't the same girl that Isra had met a year ago. Oh no, she was long gone.

"Good. You should feel bad," Isra countered in Everilda's direction. She still had her arms pressed against her chest in a rigid, irritated stance.

"Gloating much? I try to apologize and you throw me out from under you," Everilda expressed. "Anyway, I don't mean any harm. I just wanted to tell you how bad I felt. I know I acted maliciously. I tried convincing Wingdom's you were about to unleash full blown chaos—" Everilda stopped at once as she realized there was something very different about Isra, a glow that one might only experience when they were expecting a child but of course such a thing was inconceivable in the case of Isra. *No, it's something else. It's not her outer shine, but something on the inside. It goes much deeper than that. Oh goodness, no! It can't be ... can it?* Everilda mumbled to herself in thought. "Unless there was just cause for Wingdom's to have concerns?" Everilda questioned eagerly with a slightly baffled expression.

"It depends on how perceptive they are. Most are morons condemned to eternities of drudgery where they hardly ever have possession of brain cells in order to come to such conclusions," Isra said in a sharpened and brash tone.

Our Isra has gone up in the world, no longer innocent and thrust upon this ordinary human condition that the rest of us must undergo. No, she'd been touched by the darkness. There's something remarkable about the way her eyes glare upon me just a little bit more dazzling than they were before. Yes, that was it. She's tasted immortality. She's not bound to the corporeal fatality that is life anymore, Everilda thought.

"Sorry. I just can't say I am convinced by your little apology," Isra explained, looking Everilda dead in the eyes. Isra was blunt and communicated how she felt and that actuality of it was that she didn't trust Everilda at all; no matter what type of sympathetic guise she tried using.

Everilda sighed as she nodded her head. It was clear she was not the once overconfident female she used to be. Perhaps being banished and rendered mortal had done some good benefits to her personality. Maybe Everilda was seeing her life in a completely different light.

"Well, be that as it may. I just wanted to..." Everilda trailed off with a wide-eyed glance.

"Fine by me," Isra replied. "Oh, that reminds me. I have met the most intriguing of souls and he claims to know of you. Most importantly he detailed your most recent failure and how it's really not surprising. Isn't that the most peculiar thing?" Isra asked Everilda although it was more of a statement, especially in the lewd manner in which it was being retorted back to her.

"It is," Everilda answered back, carefully disregarding Isra's untactful bringing up of her misdeeds which ultimately led to her failing as a witch. Yes, Isra really wasn't one for being overly nice when she could be brutally honest.

"I'm meeting him at dusk, actually. Perhaps I will tell him that you and I conversed if only for a fleeting few minutes." Isra chortled earnestly but you could detect the glee in her voice. Oh yes, she was enjoying this, savoring it while she could because it was oh so satisfying to her.

"Yes, well. I better be off. I can't stay visible too long in certain parts of the land," Everilda explained in a hurried manner as if she was breaking boundaries just by being stood here talking to Isra.

"Oh, well then. Merry travels then. Don't get bitten by anything most awful, will you dear? Because that really would be tragic," Isra responded sardonically, evidently not caring about Everilda's apology or her entire being there in the first instance. She was far more preoccupied with her secret rendezvous with Astrid that was soon coming upon her as dusk really was only a few hours away. Isra anticipated just what wonderfully intriguing things she would find when she engaged with him again.

So really, Everilda coming here and spilling her upturned guts while pleading poverty in her holed-out rags really wasn't of any importance to Isra. Because she had moved on from that life and this was only just the beginning of a new firmly laid path that she was treading upon.

15

It wasn't quite dusk yet. The bright opaque orange sun glimmered in the distance awaiting its fiery death, but that didn't matter.

Isra was here and she couldn't resist the urge whirling around inside her head. Okay, so Astrid had said to be there exactly at dusk, but what could she say? She was curious. She couldn't wait any longer. It had been an intriguing day of beautiful learning already and with Franco imparting some wisdom her way, Isra was more than ready for this latest interaction.

But what would the beguiling Astrid turn out of his sleeve this time to impress her? Because you better believe it, Isra was more than dazzled by the brash man's interest in her and even she had to admit Astrid was rubbing off on her much more than she normally allowed a man to.

"I know I've arrived far too early but damn, I'll just sit here for a moment or two. Contain my excitement while I wait," Isra mused as she seated herself down on the grassy bank that surrounded the open-spaced ocean that was the outskirts of Seclera.

Naturally, Astrid had to pick the most risky meeting place to connect with her, but that really didn't bother Isra, for she had nothing to hide from the world. Whereas him on the other hand, she wasn't too sure about it. But Isra guessed there was plenty of time to hopefully suss the mystery man out.

Isra was getting acquainted with nature's bounty in the form of looking upon the crystal-clear turquoise-blue ocean and admiring how brilliantly calm it was. Just so peaceful and silent. The exact personality that she really admired more than anything else. It was that same moment she experienced a tap on the back of her right shoulder.

"You are way too timely for my liking!" Astrid joked as he didn't sit down beside her. He remained upright and then a very serious look resounded upon his face. "I have something to disclose in your domain. I am not sure if you will rejoice when I tell you, but tell you I must. Despite it being against the wishes of those involved, I feel you have earned this chance to know. And you are a strong, courageous woman, Isra. I know you can take this insight and find some good from it," Astrid was calm as he signaled for her to stand by waving his fingers in an upward motion.

"Come with me," he breathed, reaching for her hand as Isra rose up to his physical eye level. "We must go somewhere quiet. Isolated. Away from civilization. I know of a location perfect for just that," Astrid marveled to her with a wide-eyed grin.

"Am I going to want to stone you after this confession?" Isra asked politely, but her tone was formal and stiff, like a queen who was about to get very angry after hearing someone she believed to be loyal had indeed betrayed her.

"I would hope not," Astrid replied simply. "I am not the heel here. I am not the bad guy. I am risking every aspect of my life and limb to detail to you this grand conspiracy created in your name. Please at least allow me the reprieve by changing the sands of time in which such atrocities designed to sway you will now be completely altered. As will the fabric of reality," Astrid explained in a calm fashion, although he seemed a little anxious as his arms dropped by his shoulders whereby his hands appeared to be slightly off balance. They seemed to shake in the wind as he fought with his inner turmoil to finally tell her what he believed she should have knowledge of.

"It sounds gravely serious," Isra muttered quietly although she was dumbstruck as to what it was.

Astrid latched onto her hand, closing it upon his own and now they were running into the distance, disappearing beyond the valley of Seclera. They were almost as hidden as the moon that was now emerging, shining down, casting its reflection onto the dark murky ocean.

"It is. Now keep up, it's not far from here," Astrid instructed, dragging along with him as they passed another mass of trees.

Astrid was hurrying this along as he knew exactly where they were headed, to the so-called demonic dimension of Wretchenheart, a place long rumored to house the foulest of creatures and thus he and Isra would be not witnessed conversing there. Astrid had come to this idea via his former employer, Damien Daughtry, as he knew about the land through Damien and so it was perfect. Samuel wouldn't dare tread upon the rough terrain of Wretchenheart for he was good and pure whereas Astrid could care less. He had no fear going to places where he might encounter huge feats of danger. And taking Isra here was a big gamble indeed, but Astrid had already decided this was their best option.

So upon clicking his fingers while mumbling some well-chosen words, evidently in another language while still holding on to Isra's hand, he echoed out the sounds that would appear to be a load of gobbledygook gook because they made no sense whatsoever, but finally Astrid commanded, "Open up your wretched eternal heart and let thy cursed soul enter into your wicked breech!" leading to a big open space into the middle of nowhere which of course Isra had no recognition of because she had never set foot here before.

Isra might have guessed that this was just another part of Seclera, but she'd be wrong.

There was nothing to be seen for miles. Just a huge square of green wasteland that she imagined was cut off from the rest of the realm only distinguished by the elegantly fashioned centerpiece that stood amongst the rest of the burnt umber grassland. A tall statue of a woman, most likely a demonic sorceress or maybe it was a witch for her eyes were burning bright like rubies and her cruelly torn hollowed out heart that she held in her hand was dripping with blood. Whether it was actual blood or just part of the ornamental structure was hard to decipher, but the focal point really wasn't important.

Astrid had to halt Isra's mind fantasizing abruptly as he motioned to her. "Okay, we are here. Not a soul will hear us now. It's really crucial that you hear every single word I relay to you."

"All right. I'm listening," Isra acknowledged him.

"I lied to you when I said I didn't know much about James," Astrid began earnestly, although his head dropped to the floor; not literally, but his head hung in shame as he recalled his sordid part in the whole affair.

"You did?" Isra pressed. "I thought there was something off there. You seemed defensive."

"I know him enough to know he's part of the conspiracy. James is part of the light brigade that is solely designed to bring souls back from the dark once they have tasted it. You are enough to have them all screaming your name for you have recently turned the tide and there is a grand plan to attempt to lure you back to the good graces," Astrid explained cautiously as Isra stood taken aback at what he had said.

"Oh, I had no idea of it," Isra blundered with embarrassment; she seemed to be blushing bright red as she cupped a hand to her mouth.

"Yes, well; that's how I know of you. And your origin, to be more precise. Samuel had me stake you out from the very beginning. Ordered me to keep tabs on you but as I got to see you more, I found I was becoming fond of you. And as time withered away, I saw that you were a lot more than they had deemed you to be," Astrid explained to her truthfully.

He paused for a moment to see how Isra was taking all this. She didn't seem riled or upset at him just yet, so he saw that as a sign to continue.

"James warned me to stay away from you as did Samuel, but I didn't heed their words. I kept an eye on you closely and I watched as you discovered Everilda had betrayed you with that Jonathan fellow, who is a bloody waste of an excuse for a man, by the way," Astrid continued with a slight tinge of sarcasm.

"Yes, others have actually told me the same," Isra responded with a low gaze. She narrowed her piercing bright lime green eyes at him, getting serious as she voiced her feelings on that situation, something that she had been keeping safely under wraps within herself for a very long time now. "I don't actually know if I was in love with him or if I was just seduced by the idea of love itself, but since Jonathan is cursed and likely to remain that way for eternity, I shall never know for sure," Isra muttered although she emitted a somber rivet as if she believed the latter.

Astrid reached for Isra's chin, holding her head up high as he looked into her bewildered eyes. He was almost so close to her that he imagined kissing those scrumptiously soft lips of hers but maintaining his resilience, he refrained from doing that. *A man has to have some restraint even when he is fully enchanted by the moment and beckoned by a beautiful lady, far beyond any expectation that would dazzle the hearts of anyone,* Astrid thought to himself before he returned his focus to Isra again.

"It doesn't matter if you loved him or he loved you. He had the sheer effrontery to take on both you and Everilda at once, knowing you had some kind of endearment for him. Whether it was love or remained to be something else is not the issue here. He knew what he did was wrong and yet he still had the arrogance to carry on with the charade. I know you probably don't agree with me here, but he did you a service when you found him out for the cheating scallion he was. That gave you the opportunity to flourish and even now I still believe you don't even know just how capable you are," Astrid conveyed with honest feelings as he still had his hand holding Isra's chin up as if she should be proud to show herself off to the world.

She should not let a single thing that pathetic man did, ever darken her soul but I guess it's too late for that now. But she can still reign supreme when she discovers the truly remarkable being within herself, Astrid mused charismatically in thought.

It was true that he did really feel as if Isra should take the experience with Jonathan as a lesson and find positives from it. She had gotten away clean without too much damage being done. Okay, he had betrayed her and it was in the most hideous manner but at least she had found out sooner rather than a lot later. And really, Isra had Everilda to thank for it although she'd never have believed it.

"I guess it really doesn't add any shred of differentiation to me," Isra replied agreeing with Astrid wholeheartedly.

"Yes. I estimate it to be the exact same as you state. You are who you are going to be regardless of what torrid events shape you up into. And thus, you must remember there are things that are not always going to be within your reach. Sometimes there will be things in our lives that we have no control over but we can choose how we react to them and how they mold us into who we are," Astrid explained in a calming tone as he took his hand away from Isra's chin.

Astrid was doing his utmost in a bid to regain his focus as he so wanted to plant his lips onto hers, but that could wait. He'd have the chance to do that when she was ready. He couldn't just spring it on her now for fear she'd run in terror after all he had told her. No, he had to take baby steps and build a solid foundation of sorts before entering territory that was unknown to them both.

"But what about this whole trying to drag me back into the good graces of the goody two shoes crowd? How does that stand now?" Isra asked with sheer hunger for knowledge. Since she was veering on over sentimental reliving the Jonathan debacle, she had actually forgotten that there was a fiercely engineered plan to get her away from the darkness.

"It doesn't stand. I've told you, but more than that they'd planned for James to befriend you so while I was watching you, he was going to make contact with you and of course he has done so without question. Him and Samuel concocted an idea that you would be living in a majestic dungeon of sorts. A brilliantly thought-out chateau-like tower with the most eccentric of names. Shambre Fell."

Astrid breathed as he felt the pressure slipping away from him. The heavy burden no longer took a beating upon his weary shoulders. He felt at ease for the first time in so many moons. It was unprecedented but it felt so surreal. Astrid felt like he would have to pinch himself to believe it was finally done with but he didn't want to look foolish in front of Isra so he relented from such silly ideals.

"Oh. This goes very deep then. A murky path filled with deceit and false truths," Isra murmured in a somewhat sarcastic voice that made Astrid question for a second whether he was going to be on an even footing.

I wonder if she'll trust me after all this. I know she believes my story to be true otherwise she wouldn't be looking so indomitable but maybe she just wants to retain the complete entity of it. She's been lied to time and time again so now perhaps she just wants to hear what's really behind all the smoke and mirrors.

"It does. But I've told you. They can't do anything now I have spilled their guts to you on a metaphysical plate so to speak. I mean, have you noticed where we are?" Astrid made the suggestion to Isra which immediately made her look around.

Isra carefully observed the vicinity they were placated in with her own eyes. It wasn't exactly what you would call heavenly as she surveyed the scene around her. A quaint little statue showing a woman dripping blood down from a torn heart. No, this definitely wasn't what could be classed as enlightening. Thinking about it, Isra put her fingers to her lips in a moment of pause as she caught onto how dark it all was. All delicately tucked away in the safe curtain of the shadow. It could only mean one thing, but it couldn't be, surely?

"Yes. I do see we are not in a place of normal circumstances" Isra replied, still mesmerized by the location they were in as of this moment.

Astrid wouldn't have taken him and Isra to a demon dimension just so he could relay to her this revelation that he had decided she needed to know despite the orders of others considering against her.

Namely the light bringers and their over friendly gallant folk that likely danced around on clouds, parading around in the celestial realms, flitting between rainbows. But Astrid wasn't like them. He was not strictly considered dark but he wasn't completely light either. Perhaps it was more precise to say he was fleeting amongst the two. He was a mixed bag of emotions tinged with rebellious yearning to strike up against the light and good whereas he was deeply rooted in the occult.

"So now you see why I hauled you over here instead of the safety of the mundane earthly realm? Because they won't care to dwell here. Nobody will suspect a thing with me having the initiative to tell you in the midst of this desolate, lonely sanctuary," Astrid motioned in a serious tone.

He was giving her a forewarning glare like he was honestly being deadly pensive in his ways and means. This man wasn't kidding around with her. He'd undertaken a most risky decision in order to convey to her some truly important and also strictly illegal information obtained about her and so he had to show Isra just how really deliberate this all was.

"I do, yes," Isra responded coldly.

It wasn't actually clear why she was being so distant for a second but then Astrid saw Isra had her eyes affixed to that grotesque statue. Mostly connected to the imagery of that poor woman's soul holding her battered torn heart.

He cursed to himself in solitary thought. *Oh golly, I should have realized that would have meaning for her. She only sacrificed her broken heart the exact same way! Giving it up for damnation. Gracious, I am such an apathetic imbecile. Why didn't I even consider that maybe something like that would trigger her? Damn,* Astrid continued to holler at himself in his thoughts, clearly overreacting regarding this. He was really worried that he had indeed offended Isra whereas actually she was probably more interested in the dynamic and yet dangerous berth they were currently in.

"I hope I haven't upset you in any way. If I have, please have the gusto to let me know, otherwise I will be sure to do it again. And this pains me knowing that I may have hurt you in some manner." Astrid cut in to her, explaining his actions curtly for he was emotionally attached to this outcome. Especially if she turned away from him now after this effort he had put into his connection with her on a very profound level.

"I am not offended by you. I just find it puzzling. The light has a plan to take me back kicking and screaming and here you are taking me to places I've never laid my eyes on. It's just so ironic," Isra exclaimed meekly.

Her probing yet wary lime green eyes dropped to the desolate grassy floor in a moment in which she could only be described as losing herself in a mass of thought. Perhaps disassociating as she retreated from the world around her. Taking sanctuary within herself but she knew better than this since Astrid stood right by her and he wouldn't likely take silence for an answer.

"Is it ironic, or not so much?" Astrid asked quizzically.

His bewildering golden yellow eyes narrowed at her as if he was questioning whether she was ultimately ready for what he had at hand. The things he had designed were far greater than any feat she had accomplished and honestly now she seemed to be drifting. Even if it was ever so slightly.

"I think it could be presumed to be good. Yes, or maybe not so. I just never expected this fuss for little old me," Isra joked sardonically.

Astrid chuckled as he moved in closer to her, almost pressing himself up against her chest. He could feel her tiny yet slender frame right next to his muscular physique and he was so adjacent to her form that he was sure if he'd pressed any harder, he'd likely have crushed her precious form.

"Oh, believe me, you are more than worth the fuss," Astrid chirped as he once again resisted the urge to plant a kiss on her lips but was unable to completely tear himself away from her person without doing something gratifying.

Astrid reached for Isra's head, clasping his hands around her neck as he looked into her deep lime green eyes; and not able to thwart the attention any longer, he gently kissed her cheek.

Unknowing as to how Isra would react, Astrid kept his eyes closed for the duration of the kiss, wanting to savor this moment for all time. Opening them so that they were ajar only slightly, he caught her bemused glance staring right back at him. It wasn't one of fear and it wasn't one of terror, so he guessed it was okay. The coast was clear; well, in a manner of speaking at least.

How she didn't attempt to escape from his firm grip was beyond him but Astrid retained the satisfaction in knowing he'd had this one pure moment with her knowing that he was getting even closer to attaining the one thing he desired more than anything else. Her heart. There was literally nothing else more valuable to him.

"I was going to say something and then I lost the words," Isra stammered in the midst of awakening to the notion of his kiss.

Just being able to feel Astrid's lips on her soft opalescent skin sent chills all over her body. His hands were still clamped around her neck holding her tightly in his grasp. It had only been on the cheek but it felt magical in a way she couldn't even begin to fathom.

"You made all the lights go out. The noise just vanished from between my two ears. How did you muster such a strategic feat, Sir Astrid? You are a wonderment of wistful enchantments," Isra breathed.

"I can't say I am disappointed by all that," he mused, gently blowing warm air from his mouth onto the side of her face. "I was wondering what it would take to really have your attention. Not just have it for a minute or two, but have you completely fastened to me," Astrid chortled with sheer happiness and also a very detectable element of amusement.

"But. But..." Isra stuttered. She was uneasy. Some would say even a little bit nervous as she was shaking slightly. Her whole body was wholly vibrating with the energy generated between herself and Astrid.

"This wasn't part of the plan, was it? To seduce me," Isra breathed heavily.

She was still deeply mesmerized by that bright sheen that shone back at her in his majestic eyes. Her entire being was focused on him, glued to his fine form like a firefly would be affixed to glowing fiery orange flames.

"No, it wasn't. But we will roll with it," Astrid whispered in her ear, gently tickling her neck with his soft moist lips. He was effortless in delicately pressing them onto her immaculately flawless silky skin.

Astrid needed nothing to deter him. He craved to passionately devour her in the midst of this prestigious anarchic residence in which he planned to do a lot more than just allure her with his wicked wiles, only further coaxing her into his warm arms. But Astrid had a much sleeker plan hiding up his sleeve. Since Isra was pure at least for now, one probably wouldn't have to do much imagining to decipher exactly what that entailed.

16

Meanwhile, there was apparently an audience as a cloaked figure watched Isra and Astrid embroiled in each other's flesh. Not quite at the stage where her finely-made lace dress would be discarded on the ground as of yet, but close enough to signify that Isra would not be maidenly for much longer. However, as the mystery soul let down their dark black hood revealing a head of mousy brown hair it was clear as to who it was.

It was comical really; you honestly had to laugh as James scowled at Astrid from his safe place neatly tucked afar from where Astrid was slowly devouring Isra. James had cleverly followed Astrid as he'd led Isra astray with him. Only the raven man had no knowledge of it. For if he had, Astrid would have surely scolded James or pecked his eyeballs out. Whichever way you looked at it, Astrid would have been furious if he had known.

Stupidly, Astrid had made the assumption that no member of the light would dare tread here for it was not a spiritual paradise. In fact, it was quite the opposite when you noted that Astrid had picked a demon dimension to have his nefarious way with Isra. Of course, the idea to come to Wretchenheart had come from Damien Daughtry, Astrid's former employer and loyal friend, who had suggested that

Astrid confess all to Isra in a place where heavenly eyes would not beseech them.

"Well, she evidently won't be a virgin for much longer. Look at him go. He's not hesitating for a moment," James muttered to himself while observing Astrid giving Isra his full attention. James took due care to ensure he was not overheard as that would have been awkward to say the least.

Just the thought of Astrid peeling himself away from Isra, all naked and brandishing his manly parts was enough to make James shudder, especially if Astrid had decided that being unclothed added no barrier to a full-blown fiery confrontation with his nemesis of sorts.

No, that's an image I don't need to see, James professed in his thoughts.

Ultimately James had followed Astrid here to see if there was a danger of which he would need to relay a very crucial revelation depicting Astrid's antics back to the overlord of enlightenment himself. It was now apparent that James would have to do just that, even if only in a desperate attempt to reclaim some shards of this disenchantment mission.

"That's it then. I have to tell Samuel all of this. Goodness save me, for he will not be best pleased. Not only has our sneaky Astrid tempted our flighty dark enchantress with his willful self but now he's intending to take her innocence as well. Nope, Samuel will not be amused at all," James retorted sarcastically. "He really knows how to take literally every single thing to the next level, doesn't he?" James professed, again in a sarcastic nature.

Yes, there was no getting away from the internal truth. James was going to have to go running all the way to Samuel.

17

____

Samuel knew he'd be in for an arduous morning, already having a fresh cup of steaming hot coffee placed on his desk next to him. It was a bright, breezy day and the morning was more than welcoming to him as the sun streamed in through his office château windows making the transparent panes of glass sparkle in the morning glow. However, just as Samuel was about to pick up his coffee cup to take a most needed sip, James strode into his office with a furrowed brow.

It was clear the spiritual soul was troubled over something and Samuel began to rethink the term grueling intensely, since whatever was about to unleash from James was surely not going to impress him. With the morbid assumption as to what was going on Samuel didn't waste any time. Samuel just came out with it because he honestly suspected the worst.

"Dare I even ask you what's come down?" Samuel muttered. His lips were pursed as he was about to take a sip from his hot caffeinated beverage. But he held it in anticipation of what he might hear in revelation.

James acknowledged Samuel with a long drawn-out sigh. Evidently James had not slept as he slumped into the chair abutting

Samuel's desk. "Dare might be a derogatory term, but I appreciate the sentiment. It's been a rough day and it hasn't even begun properly yet."

"Would you like some coffee? I am going to go out on a limb and assume you have not slept!" Samuel offered although his line of questioning was more of an interrogation than an offer as a tired James could only mean a very dire situation that was filled with exhaustion. And as tremendous as it was to think that this might simply be the angelic fellow falling into the insomniac trap with overworking himself to the brink, Samuel knew better.

James wasn't too careful as he stifled a yawn before his eyes fell upon Samuel in a dead stare, not even bothering to take much effort to ensure his tiredness was noted. This only fueled Samuel's suspicions. *I already know I am not going to derive pleasure from whatever our young handsome James has to relay, but the more I observe from him, the more concern I have. He's not even trying to conceal it, for goodness sakes. It's clear something big has commenced but just what I am not too clear on as of yet,* Samuel mumbled to himself in his thoughts.

"You might want to sit yourself down. You won't like what I am going to inform you of," James started with an awkward glance, one that emitted nervousness and also the slight tinge of fear.

"Oh golly, now what?" Samuel exclaimed although at this point, he was feeling pretty calm which was ironic considering what he was about to hear.

"I am sitting down, boy. Just tell me already!" Samuel responded. He was growing impatient with James. It was noticeable in the way the light bringer tapped his fingers on his desk in a repetitive fashion, obviously waiting for James to just hurry up and say whatever it was.

"It's Astrid!" James blurted out. *Fuck it. That wasn't so bad was it?* he chortled in thought. *Now we have to get to the part where he's completely lost the plot. Astrid has trashed our entire mission or should I say yours and he's really rubbing the shit in our faces.*

Samuel took yet another huge deluge of coffee because he had a feeling what was coming next. The heated beverage travelled down his throat at lightning speed, not making any haste in slowing down as evidently Samuel was stressed. He didn't even savor the bitter flavor, just let it go straight down.

Oh, just wait for it. Just fucking don't even delay it anymore. I knew he was up to something. His absences were getting far too frequent for my liking but come on let's have it, the light bringer chorused with a sarcastic rage in his head. "Oh, good heavens, what the hell has he done now?" Samuel exclaimed.

"Where do I start? It's much worse than we could have ever anticipated," James confessed although he wasn't sure how to begin. His expression was one of shock and perplexity because James really didn't know just how Samuel would react, but stalling wouldn't make the detailing of it any easier. It was better to just spew it out even if it did feel like James was vomiting some vile spew of some kind. At least verbally anyhow.

"How about you just contain yourself for a moment. Take some caffeine into you and then we try this again," Samuel mused although there was an angry descent in his tone. But nevertheless Samuel passed James his own mug of coffee and waited while James took a huge gulp of the steaming brown liquid before passing Samuel his coffee back to him.

"Thank you. I really needed that. Okay, back to business," James excused himself, before wiping some coffee away from the side of his mouth. "Astrid has told Isra all about us. The mission to bring her back into the good graces of the light. Everything, really. He's really blown the water on this one and then some," James explained.

"Oh, did he now?" Samuel inquired although it was more rhetorical than an actual question.

Samuel resisted the strong pulsating urge to pound his fist upon his desk and instead began eagerly rubbing his hands together in a prayer-like stance. A feeble attempt to stay grounded, some would say, but Samuel had to do something before he overreacted and went absolutely batshit crazy over all of this turbulence.

"Yes, I am afraid it is so. But there's more..." James precluded earnestly, not wanting to hold back because he knew it was better to just get on with it. *The sooner I tell him, the faster he can go mental over it and then I'm in the clear because I delivered the goods,* James conferred to himself in his head as he was strategically planning all of his game plan out. Step by step.

"Go on," Samuel encouraged. Again, Samuel still seemed incredibly calm. Evidently James did not see the rage that Samuel was holding inside of himself.

"He's.... erm......" James stammered and stumbled. "Oh dear, how the hell do I even say this?" James mumbled. He was nervously letting his handshake but honestly it was out of his control. It wasn't that James was fearful, you understand, but more worried of the outburst that was soon to be coming any minute.

"Just bloody say it! Your impetuousness is driving me crazier by the second!" Samuel scolded him with a sneeringly hard-faced stare.

"Astrid is human now," James blurted out. He blushed a little as this part of the little conundrum was the one that nobody on this grand earth was ever expecting.

Samuel didn't take his eyes off James. Not able to contain the fury inside him any longer, he thumped his fist upon his desk, slamming it down. The sound was so loud that James really wanted to cover his ears but such an action would likely provoke Samuel, as he'd probably find it extremely impolite. Samuel nursed his bruised fist for a second before returning to the grim reality he now resided in.

"What in the deathly abyss are you even talking about? Are you sure it's even the same Astrid? Good heavens, James explain this to me," Samuel ranted before he surged into an impending fit of anger. "NOW!" Samuel barked.

"I don't know how Astrid got to be a human but I know it's him. His attitude isn't one that you'd really forget in a hurry," James explained quickly, for Samuel was only going to get more riled if he wasn't snappy with it.

"No, it isn't," Samuel concurred. Some of his aggression dwindled slightly as the realization dawned upon him that James was indeed telling the truth.

"He taunted me. Told me very explicitly he was going to have his merry way with Isra and that I wouldn't be able to do a thing about it. He even dared me to tell you about it," James continued.

"Yes, that's his usual brash way so I can't imagine him being anything else. Please continue," Samuel urged. He waved his hands apart as if to signal that James was okay to go on with this without the fear he would be reprimanded because of it.

"As I stated, there is more. He was already devouring her when I got there. To Wretchenheart, where I caught him in the midst of deflowering Isra and it was a most graphic image indeed," James finished, not wanting to beat about the bush. It was better to just be honest even if the truth was hard to accept.

It was at this moment that Samuel had just taken in a huge sip of his now lukewarm coffee when he stopped at once unable to stop himself. It was inevitable it would go down this way as Samuel's face were frozen as if he was some kind of solid stone statue. Clearly the shock was too much for Samuel to take in. He involuntarily spat dark brown liquid all over himself and his desk as he spluttered it like liquidated spew. The murky colored bitter beverage had utterly soaked Samuel's wooden desk, also reducing some written papers to mush as it saturated everything.

"You have got to be fucking joking? He's done *what*?" Samuel screeched. He was unable to believe what he was hearing.

"He's taken Isra's virginity. And in a demon dimension of all places," James muttered in a somewhat sardonic manner, as he was hinting at something that Samuel hadn't quite grasped yet.

"Yes. Wretchenheart. I know of it. It's not somewhere any of us can safely tread. You took great risks to spy on him with her over there, didn't you?" Samuel asked with eager fascination but the way he sat back in his red velvet armchair with his eyes glued to James and his hands pressed together suggested he was in a deep thinking pose.

James eyed Samuel seriously for a second before answering him. "Yes well, he seems to have a benign obsession with her. I didn't want to go there but I never thought he'd have taken it to such an extreme."

Samuel nodded in agreement as he had known about this for

much longer than James, having already witnessed it first-hand with Astrid's inexplicable behavior when it came to the lady in question. But taking her innocence along with destroying their well-planned and established mission was a step too far. Samuel cursed in his head as he couldn't get his mind around the fact that Astrid really had well and truly messed this one up real good this time.

"This is an infatuation that has been occurring for a while," Samuel coaxed gently. "Do I need to know the exact entity of what he said to her?" Samuel asked James although he was certain he was already in possession of the answer.

"He said that we have been trying to bring her to the light. That we orchestrated and ordained a divine plan which of course is true."

"That it is," Samuel agreed.

"Astrid named you and me as the ones behind it all. He also said it wouldn't mean anything now he has relayed it to her. He also said to her she has great potential and that he believes she is worth the fuss being made over her," James commented which only spurred Samuel on to believe that this was more serious than he expected.

"Yes, so he's trashed our entire assignment then?" Samuel pondered although he had a sneaking feeling he already knew the answer here.

"I'm afraid so," James motioned.

Samuel sank back further in his armchair, pressing his back fully against it as if it was providing some comfort of some kind. He sat with a moody looking glance that was both thoughtful and perplexing to James but the reality dawned upon Samuel. This time he couldn't just lecture Astrid and let him off with a warning. No, he'd crossed the line here and it was time for the light bringer to be a lot tougher.

"And after all I've done for him, he betrays me and the light in this despicable manner. Well, at least we know where we stand in his mindset, but it's not enough. I have to deal with Astrid myself and I know there is only one way this can go. I'll have to show him that I am the authority figure in this vicinity. It's about time I let Astrid know just who he is messing with."

Samuel reflected before taking a pause as remembered a crucial detail he had neglected to mention. He figured that Astrid would likely still be in Wretchenheart, but perhaps this matter could indeed wait until tomorrow for Samuel had some other things to take care of before his very personal interaction with the former raven.

"I shall deal with Astrid," Samuel commanded James with a stern yet serious tone.

The spiritual man was being very clear to point out that Astrid was not getting away with this one. Oh no, he'd be in for it now. Too much had occurred in Samuel's wake for Astrid to just get away clean. No, swift action would have to be taken. Samuel knew exactly what it would take but that could wait for now. Other business they had to contend with would have to come first and foremost.

Let's see; breaking confidentiality against bearers of the light to dark souls, check. Leaking concealed prophecies to the subjects of said foretelling. Double check. Poking his beak into things that didn't concern him; well fuck me, damn. That was going to be another tick, wasn't it?

"Deal with him? He seems to get off scot-free every single time." James probed, having already caught sight of much of Astrid's bizarre action taking more times than he cared to count.

"Trust me, I shall deal with him," Samuel affirmed. "I know you have your grievances with him, but it appears I have been too much of a father figure to the boy. Man or raven. However it is. But I know in order to fully exact my presence in this establishment I must become tougher on him. Being resilient is difficult at the best of times but in my line of work it certainly doesn't help when I have an emotional attachment to one of my employees. I've always drawn the line with Astrid. I've let his misdemeanors slip. I have always let it go thinking he'd get better overtime or find something more worthwhile to put that pent up rage of his into but the truth of it is, he's only got worse. That's my fault. I blame myself for how torrid it's gotten over these years. But I always believed he'd improve somewhat," Samuel confessed in a long drawn-out tone. He pressed his hands to his forehead, closing his eyes for a moment before opening them again suddenly.

The light bringer was prompt in turning around to face James. He displayed a furrowed brow sort of glance, and then Samuel requested to James, "Do you think you could reach the 'on high' for me? I need them to carry out something and I have very little time to conduct it myself. Do you think you could endeavor to do that for me?"

"Sure, no problem," James responded before turning to leave. "Although I have to say, something drastic has to be done and fast if we are to stop him in time."

Of course, James was pertaining to Astrid and whatever designs he had in mind in regards to Isra and her dark fervor. Because surely he wasn't stopping at just taking her virginity. No, Astrid was a man of passion and danger and whatever he had up his sleeve was sure to rile everyone when they discovered the full extent of just what he had been up to.

"It will be done, all right. That much I can assure you of," Samuel commented, sitting up in his armchair. He looked triumphant as he had a smile on his face for the first time in a while. It was refreshing to see. Almost like it was a sign that things were about to come to a head, a positive resolution. A conclusion to this big mess was about to be reached for all concerned.

Well, maybe not so in the case of Astrid but at this stage of the game he was of the least importance.

"If you happen to find the scrawny bastard before I do, tell him if he's in for one hell of a spanking. Oh, and don't pardon the expression as on this occasion I could be meaning the literal," the light bringer joked before retaining his serious forewarning glare as he returned his attention to James.

Laying his bold blue eyes onto the angelic warrior's carefully, Samuel instructed James very clearly. "Oh, and once you have relayed the news to the 'on high' and have the permissions granted and finalized, please understand my meaning when I say this. You are not to intervene any further. Not with Isra. And most definitely not with Astrid. I will undertake it upon myself to deal with this matter personally. I am the only one that can. I'm the one Astrid has the issue with. It's my supremacy and my allegiance that he is violating of his own free will. So it is I that must overrule him."

Samuel veered his eyes out upon the land that lay beyond his glass encased office. Noting that Shambre Fell was prominently visible amongst all of that mass of greenery. That tower spiking up into the sky like a forbidden fortress that could only be discovered by those that possessed the sight to view it. It was then that Samuel had the most brilliant idea.

"Oh, if he wants to play, we shall go along with his little game. But I'll beat him at it by putting yet another obstacle in his path," Samuel chuckled to himself as he continued to admire the view.

18

It was already getting to dusk and Astrid was growing impatient. Standing at the top of the cliff peak that dominated the mystery land of Glamvein, he had been awaiting her arrival for almost an hour now. Yet again, she was taking her sweet time, most likely stopping along, smelling every single rose that she came across. Or was that too presumptuous? Damn, he cared less. He'd been incredibly intimate with Isra in the physical sense so he was hoping the ice that normally stood between them would be thinner than usual.

Since their last meeting in Wretchenheart, Astrid had decided upon himself that bringing Isra back to the site where she'd first experienced her entry into darkness would maybe inspire some creativity within her. He wanted to harness her power. Astrid was determined to let Isra fully explore her melancholic self, only not for her to not slip into that demonic depressing despair that normally came with the pressure of having such an intense presence like the one that Isra laid claim to.

Finally, there was a glimmer in the distance. A shiny white, almost golden-highlighted head bobbed up and down as it edged closer to the mountain peak. This was only further enhanced by the

151

midnight velvet blue that covered the entrancing slim figure that was emerging right before Astrid. Isra could only stand back in amusement as Astrid frowned at her. Almost like he was silently growling. Evidently, he was not amused by her tardiness, but still she had to laugh at him. For no man was the boss of her.

"You are late," Astrid warned with a cautious stare.

His glowing golden eyes burned into hers, complementing the fiery lime green that resided in them as her face remained one of sheer entertainment. Isra was not put off by his fierce look that he threw at her. She couldn't help but feel like he was reminding her of a stern schoolteacher about to give her a lavish reprimand. The thought amused her greatly.

Still laughing at him, Isra replied simply, "Ah yes, sorry. I was enjoying the view as I walked here."

"Smelling the roses, no doubt," Astrid remarked at her with a coy look. *And why does that not surprise me?* he chuckled to himself in thought. *I knew she'd be dawdling along. Smelling the freaking roses and no doubt making merry fun out of it as she discovered yet another piece of nature's glory.*

"In a manner of speaking. Quite possibly," Isra answered. She was being cryptic, not really letting on to what had kept her so long and not really giving him any insight into her current mindset because honestly she believed it would be more fun for Astrid to try and fathom her out. "Anyhow, I've given what you told me a lot of thought. Ironed out everything precisely and I realize this may come across as rude, but I've been wondering what you'll gain out of all this? Relaying it all to me. Destroying someone's grand plan because now I am aware of it? I mean really, what do you get out of it all? I am curious. Please enlighten me." Isra questioned him with pursed lips. Her stance was standoffish as she kept her distance from him, maintaining a look of disbelief as she awaited him to answer her.

"What do I gain out of it? Are you serious?" Astrid glowered at her with fury. "I've given you everything you need to break out on your own and not have the love and light brigade keeping tabs on you.

And you suddenly wonder what the hell I am going to get out of it?" Astrid beseeched her, unable to believe what he was hearing.

"There's no need to get flustered. I just had an inquisitiveness about it. It's not often you find someone who is willing to go to such lengths to relay something when there is not something involved for them," Isra explained although she felt like she had offended Astrid in some way. Clearly, he was taking this personally but she didn't often trust people, if ever. With anything so she felt like she had the right to ensure that she had his assurance.

"I'm not getting unhinged with you here, girl. But I've given you everything. Can't you see where we are?" Astrid pointed out to her as he was hoping the location would jog Isra's memory to a fairly recent iconic event that took place here.

"I appreciate it. It's just I seldom trust folk these days. I seem to get overly burned whenever I do," Isra retorted in an icy tone.

Okay, I knew this was a trust issue, but surely she must be able to know who I am by now. If I was to drag her into a slaven pit of treacherous wolves, I would have done it before now! But is it ever enough for her? Astrid pursued nonchalantly in his thoughts.

"I don't intend any offence directed at your personage here. It's just I don't know if I can believe that you don't gain anything from my knowledge of such valuable information," Isra continued, only succeeding to rile Astrid's fury even more as she did so. "I am sure you wouldn't normally care for the existence of someone like myself. You strike me as the self-important type that meanders through life helping yourself to the ripe fruits on the scrumptious and plump tree but once someone else comes along, you can't help but make sure they have no scraps left to savor. I mean, you did get to have me in a very sexual manner," she commented, reminding him that they had in fact communed together in an intimate way.

It was something she had never done with another man, not even the pathetic weasel Jonathan. But Astrid couldn't help but take offence to what Isra said. Her words stuck in his throat like acid burning away ever so slowly but not swift enough to take away the scalding pain from when one needed to vomit quickly. This only added more salt to the ever-impending open wound that Astrid was finding extremely impeccable to ignore.

Astrid glared at her with fierce bewildering red grisliness residing in the pits that were normally his eyes. As red as fresh blood. Astrid was putrid with envy and he was perhaps a little bit annoyed by this bewildering yet dark enrapturing queen of the night that he had come to know. Surely by now he'd have been able to tolerate her bold and brash insults and unappreciative standoffish demeanor but no, Isra was pissing him off no end.

"You know, could you show me some appreciation? A scrap of it wouldn't go amiss here. I can get banished for telling you this. Samuel would have my head on a golden platter if he ever found out what I'd done pertaining to you," Astrid announced to her with a harsh yet cold stare. *This woman is driving me crazy. She's so damn stubborn. So full of it, so full of wit and all those elemental charms but when it comes to it, she just won't budge an inch, oh no,* he cursed to himself in sardonic thought.

Isra lifted her head in flaring interest all of a sudden. Samuel? Now where had she heard that name before?

"Samuel?" she inquired with a piercing look. The sharp emerald green in her eyes tinged a slight lighter color for a second as her mind raced.

Oh shit, Astrid stopped himself in thought. *I've done it again. Good golly, I have got to get more control on my emotions. For heaven's sake Astrid, get it together.* "Samuel, the light bringer. And James who is fast becoming an enemy of mine. And they are certainly not folks you need to be concerned about," Astrid sniped through gritted teeth.

Astrid was still rather hacked off with her and now he was showing it even though he knew it would likely cause further issues. It was a disappointment for Astrid as he had hoped Isra would at least deliver on the goods so all this salivating would be worth it. He'd had his heart set on the witch for so long that now he was starting to feel like a fiendish stalker. Astrid had slept and breathed Isra for so many moons now, and it was starting to take a toll on him. The specks of silvery gray in his hair were more prominent than ever in his human form. It appeared that he had even begun to grow a beard which was also gray like the hair that had managed to grow upon his head.

"You have enemies? How interesting," Isra retorted.

The witch turned her back to him, leaving only her long golden curls in his view. Her long tresses of hair dominated her slender frame as they descended down her blue cloak. Again, she was giving him short answers. The iciness in her voice was really starting to grate on him.

"Well yes, doesn't every soul?" he snapped back, lowering his voice quickly at the last second as he knew he had to change the tact. Especially if he was to get anywhere with her.

"Calm yourself, dear. I only meant that I thought you were more of the do-gooder kind." Isra laughed as she turned her head around so fast her long golden hair could have smacked the tempestuous Astrid in the face. And he was being so rude toward her that he may well have deserved it.

What in the devil? Astrid mocked to himself in thought, almost chuckling in bemused thought. *She thinks I am one of those love and light types? Please girl, you have no freaking idea just what I am capable of. I may be connected to those who walk in the light but I have always been attracted to the darker side of life.* "I can assure you I am no do-gooder," he recited with confidence. The hilarity of it was clearly visible upon his face. It really was quite amusing to him that she would think that of him.

"Good to know, because if I ever get a whim to unleash chaos upon this grim, dreary world, I may just invite you to join me!" Isra cajoled at him with a wink before she turned to him, eyeing him up as her eyes lingered upward alongside the rest of her body. She graciously planted a kiss upon his forehead, giggling like a virginal schoolgirl as she brushed past him without a care.

Astrid was so dazed by her gratifying gesture that he barely caught sight of his surroundings, never mind what Isra was doing. Sinking into a self-imposed coma, he closed his eyes to savor it. He was so stuck in the aroma of that kiss. The sweet notes of rose that hummed around his senses. Also, the sweet stickiness from her lips reminded him of honey.

"I'd be very receptive to the invitation. And believe me; I've long wanted a decent excuse to do just that, girl..." He trailed off as he realized once again he was alone. Isra was nowhere to be seen. She'd disappear quicker than lightning, once again eluding him. "Bloody scheming enchantress!" he cursed after her, but of course, she was long gone so she would not have heard his frustration.

19

Astrid hadn't seen Isra since she had vanished from him only a few minutes ago, but he suspected that he'd be seeing her again soon enough so it only made sense to continue on. In order to deliver on his promise to Rhiannon meant beckoning a journey that he must undertake in order to fulfill that.

He had to admit Isra's behavior was puzzling. Astrid had connected with her in no way another man ever had. He'd made love to her and he'd seen the parts of herself that she dared not show to anyone else. Astrid felt like he was inevitably closer to Isra than ever before but still she was very hard to work out. Her standoffish demeanor was peculiar to say the least but perhaps she just simply had a lot of trust issues to heal from. Maybe she didn't believe that Astrid had good intentions at heart for her even after all he had told her and shown her in his endearing yet very practical manner.

However, Astrid wasn't going to let this sway him. Unbeknownst to Isra, Astrid had a preexisting engagement but since he was about to meet someone very familiar to Isra, he wasn't about to tell her as to whom or what that was. So making haste, Astrid ventured out of Glamvein heading toward his destination, a quaint little village that reminded Astrid of something you'd expect to see in a fairyland.

Rainfur was a host to those who believed solely in the beauty of nature and love and light. It housed witches, wiccans, pagans and many more besides.

And it really wasn't surprising to him that the notorious vagrant Everilda Daughtry had found herself a home here. *And likely some hovel close to the dirt,* Astrid remarked to himself in a somewhat sardonic tone.

Yes, it really wasn't the best location for someone like Everilda but she always had brass balls even after being banished so Astrid could understand why she chose to dwell here instead of a million other domiciles. Getting caught wasn't really a fear for her since she rejoiced in the attention she got.

The good news was that Rainfur, the country-like village where Everilda was currently living; wasn't that far away from Glamvein. In fact, Astrid would be able to go straight to Shambre Fell afterward since it was only a stone's throw away from the extraordinary land that Samuel had conjured up out of nothing. For some reason he felt like Isra might be there. It was a thought he couldn't shake but yet had to take it as a possible premonition since he knew the witch was still undecided about whether to take up residence there.

It took him a while but even at a steady pace, Astrid found himself greeted by a series of local fruit bearing trees. A beautiful enormous tree with round juicy oranges was the first one he came across and while he resisted the urge to help himself to one of the tasty citrus fruits, he soon found himself next to an abundant cherry tree. *Oh, can you imagine the irony since most of the wiccans were probably virgins,* Astrid chuckled to himself in his thoughts. *But it's the most exquisite touch.*

Coming closer to the scorched land in Rainfur that had evidently been burned to a crisp many years or perhaps even centuries ago; the exact timing of this event was not known. But it was said that the village had to be replenished from scratch and every single crop replanted as if it was a completely brand-new land, as though the disastrous event had never ever happened.

But those details were only minor to Astrid; he was visiting

Everilda for a very specific reason. Namely because he had promised the demoness Rhiannon that he would indeed reunite her with her estranged earthly daughter. But naturally, Everilda had no idea of the fact so this would indeed be a most riveting meeting. I mean, she'd had no real knowledge of her father Damien either, except that he had vanished when she was very young so as far as Everilda was concerned there was nothing for her to know regarding her parental guardians.

Finally, coming up to the gray stone path, Astrid braced himself as he knocked on the door. He took sight of the mucky glass window panes that clearly hadn't been given a good sparkling clean for a very long time. It was safe for him to assume that Everilda would be of a similar appearance but only time would tell. Astrid was still standing there, having tapped his fist upon the wooden door and alas, no answer. Feeling impatient and having a schedule, he lunged his fist upon the door yet again.

This time he heard movement from the inside of the cottage. Small footsteps were pacing around quickly in an effort to come towards the door. Astrid didn't even need the indicator to know any different but Everilda was anxious. The door swung open at last and a face was eerily peering over at Astrid that was only distinguished by her dirty golden blonde hair that hung down past her shoulders. Her forlorn face only further highlights just how wretched her physical appearance was since leaving the stately privileges of Wingdom's Academy.

It was all living large and in a fine established castle like fortification but as soon as that was taken away, Everilda had evidently been reduced to wearing sodden rags and hadn't been taking much care of her skin either.

Everilda gave Astrid an incredulous look, glaring at him intensely but this didn't bother Astrid that much.

Astrid had actually expected Everilda to be defensive so when she asked him rather rudely without warning, "Who the devil are you? And what are you doing on my pathway?" Astrid didn't take offense to it. He took it like a man and without prejudice because he was about to rip her world apart. It felt like the courteous and considerate thing to do but it wasn't about to change why he was here so he decided to be strictly business with Everilda since she likely didn't trust him very much. Or at all.

"Hello. I am Astrid. I am a friend of your father, Damien. Please can I come in?" Astrid requested to her in a sincere voice.

Yes, he knew he was being friendly to Isra's nemesis but his loyalty to Damien Daughtry went far beyond a vendetta between two teenage women. Astrid hoped Isra would indeed understand what it meant for someone like him to communicate with someone he didn't really know because of a connection with another person.

Astrid wanted Isra to comprehend that just because he was engaging with Everilda, someone of whom Isra hated no less, didn't mean he was being disrespectful toward her. He would have to explain himself to Isra soon enough and take his lumps if he had to in regard to him conversing with the enemy.

"My father? I haven't seen him in years. How could you possibly know him?" Everilda inquired in a tone that could emit pure disbelief.

Astrid took a breath. He knew this part would be difficult. Perhaps Everilda would not take him seriously but there were far greater forces at work here. Everilda clearly had no clue about her actual heritage other than what she had heard from her mother Damaris, or should we say false mother since Rhiannon was Everilda's real mother, but that was a more complicated facet to go through. Still there was plenty of time to mull over everything.

"Look, I know it's hard to comprehend Everilda, but I do know your father. In fact, I have spoken with him. There are prying eyes in these parts please let me in so we can discuss this in a safe environment." Astrid appealed to her in an earnest manner.

By prying eyes he meant spies such as Samuel and James who would no doubt be looking into his ins and outs since he had left their good graces. Well, not that he had officially turned his back on the light, but since James knew it would only be a matter of time in Astrid's opinion so he had to work quickly. And he certainly didn't need anyone catching him in a complex rendezvous with Everilda, a banished witch that had a reputation that went far beyond her tarnished name.

Everilda pressed her nose past the door, barely leaving it ajar she squinted across at the area surrounding her homely terrain. Her eyes ventured past the scorched grass land and then amongst the neighboring fruit trees before she returned her attention to Astrid.

"Okay, fine. Come in. Be warned it's not the most accommodating of abodes but it does me nicely." Everilda moaned as she opened the door for her house guest before giving the location outside another, going over with her eyeballs just to ensure there was nobody creeping around. Watching her.

"I've probably seen worse in my tenure," Astrid commented as he walked in through the narrow passageway of Everilda's home.

Everilda was right; her home was an absolute hell hole closely resembling a burnt-out barn yard or something similar in nature. Astrid didn't really know if there was anywhere to be seated so he just stood against the fireplace which was also dismal, just a simple black ebony fireplace that was lit well with bright orange flames. A nice touch for a place dominated by plain gray walls.

And Astrid was right to assume whether there was anything suitable to sit on as Everilda pointed at a dirty brown-colored armchair that looked like it hadn't been washed in centuries. The gray stone floor would likely be cleaner so Astrid declined.

"Erm, no. I'd rather sit on the floor. But thank you for the generosity. Listen, I know this will be an awkward discussion so I'm going to get the elephant out of the room so to speak," Astrid recited to Everilda, who looked stalwart, just stood there by her brown armchair as though she wanted to say something but instead remained mute. "I've not only been in contact with your father, but..." Astrid stammered halfway as he realized Everilda would not be able to take this information in. He wondered how she'd react other than shouting and calling him a prevaricator but Astrid figured he had to try because there was no other alternative.

"But what?" Everilda finished Astrid's sentence for him. She was edging on precarious as she eyed him, giving him the most dicey stare she could have possibly mustered.

"There is no easy way to say this but I've been in contact with your mother!" Astrid blurted out, taking note of his subject for any sudden psychotic reactions since this was likely a trigger for her.

Everilda had suffered abandonment because of her father and Damaris wasn't really a strong pivotal figure in Everilda's life. Even through her childhood into her early teens, Damaris had paid very little attention to Everilda because she shied away from anything remotely dark, never mind a demonic descendant. Of course, Damaris had known since Rhiannon had performed the curse that led to Everilda's conception at Damaris and Damien's wedding ceremony even though Damaris had physical relations with Damien and also gave birth to Everilda, she knew deep down in the metaphysics: Everilda belonged to Rhiannon. So you could say that Damaris shunted Everilda.

And it was also likely that Everilda resented Damaris because of it, although she had no inclination of the mortal's reasoning for such a choice.

"My mother?" Everilda gasped. She sounded flabbergasted like she could not conceive of such a notion appearing in the conversation. Or maybe it was disbelief, who knew?

"Not, Damaris," Astrid corrected, almost instantly, which was likely to throw Everilda for a loop since that was the answer she expected him to expel out of his mouth.

"Erm .... who then??" Everilda stuttered. Her eyes shifted nervously which made Astrid incredibly uncomfortable as he had no idea how she would react when he told her the real truth.

"Sit down," Astrid commanded.

Everilda sank slowly down in her murky brown armchair despite the anxiety and confusion she felt all around her. "So if it's not my mother then what or whom exactly are you referring to?" Everilda quizzed him with a peculiar look.

She clearly didn't trust Astrid as her eyes burned into him, studying him very closely. When you think about it, she'd invited this stranger into her home and he was now telling her some strange complexity that she didn't have any understanding of.

Astrid began slowly, being very articulate to convey his meaning in a concise and crystal-clear manner because this would be one hell of a bomb he would be unleashing upon Everilda's domain. "Everilda, do you have any knowledge of your father's life before he met your mother?" Astrid asked carefully.

He looked into her eyes and anyone would have been able to decipher that he was being honest. The way those golden yellow eyes of his darkened in the middle of his pupils showed he was being authentic with her. The irony of this was Everilda didn't like this one bit and this made her have even more concerns over this man Astrid that had just stumbled upon her out of nowhere.

"No. None whatsoever," Everilda answered him simply.

"Okay, well, he summoned a demon called Rhiannon," Astrid replied. He took a pause before he took it upon himself to carry on with the rest because it was sure to be a projectile of an adumbration. "Together they launched a renegade against Wingdom's Academy, the very same establishment that recently expelled you. But Rhiannon grew on your father Damien in a destructive way. Your father was obsessed with Rhiannon and even after the curse she placed on all female souls that entered Wingdom's Academy he still found he could not let go of her. But your paternal grandmother Marie tried to block this horrific connection between your father and Rhiannon. It resulted in him being betrothed to Damaris, your supposed mother, but Rhiannon stormed the wedding and it was there and then that she..." Astrid cut off abruptly as he realized Everilda was completely silent.

Not a single word escaped from her lips. Unfounded as it was, it was indeed true.

"She announced to the entire congregation that their first-born child would be hers, truly. Theorizing a curse in a sense but she was being literal. You are that child, Everilda," Astrid confessed bluntly, only when his eyes met Everilda's, she wasn't brazen. Or brimming with anger as he expected to be. *How very peculiar,* the raven mused to himself in his thoughts. *Why does she not want to rip my head off? That is most unusual.*

Actually, Everilda didn't seem at all surprised by this news as she appeared to have a smile resounding on her face. A rare notion for this witch or former, since she was rarely happy. Ever.

"Interesting," was all that came out of Everilda's mouth in reply. It was though she had a sneaking suspicion about something and now Astrid had provided some confirmation to her.

"Is that all?" he asked her quizzically. "I just told you that your mother you believed to be so is not actually your mother."

"Yes, you did but it's always puzzled me why my mortal mother never really liked or even loved me," Everilda mumbled. "I was always so wrong to her. It didn't matter what I did or how good I was, she would always find fault in something. I thought honestly for so many years that it was me. I disappointed her so badly that she had no choice but to reject me, but now I understand. It has all become clear," Everilda concurred in a very formal yet honest way like she was communicating to an old friend instead of a stranger that stood in her living area.

"I see," Astrid muttered back to her. He narrowed his eyes at Everilda very conspicuously as if he regarded her as something out of this outlandish universe for yet again there was no overheated reaction. "You know..." he stared at her in a low voice. "I feel a bit disappointed here. After all I've told you, I was expecting some fireworks," Astrid joked in her direction.

"Sorry to not be of service," Everilda countered sardonically. "Perhaps you can tell me some more about my mother and then maybe explosions may resurface," Everilda replied sharply as though she was addressing a subject of hers.

"Well, she's a demoness," Astrid began earnestly. "Very powerful and very volatile which explains you rather well in the past, don't you think? You've always had a bit of uptightness about you. A fiery temper which explains why things with your former friend Isra went rather sour."

One might have wondered how Astrid knew all that but since

Everilda was desperate to get the goods of this conversation she refrained from dragging herself into low vibrational territory. As far as she was concerned, the thing with Isra was done. There was nothing else to say. I mean, she'd tried and Isra had practically thrown it back in her face while mocking Everilda for having the gusto to do it so what use would that be? No, it was over. Finished. It was doubtful Isra would ever change how she saw Everilda now even with an awakening of sorts since she left the finery behind her.

Oh no, Isra is far too set in her ways to even acknowledge the potentiality that I may have changed. No, best to leave things as they are, Everilda chorused to herself in her thoughts.

"A demoness, huh? Intriguing, I must say, but why has she never been with me?" Everilda asked Astrid, pressing the inquiry even further.

Everilda was summarizing this inside her head so intensely to the point her brain might explode if she kept on with it but her point was justified. It was all well and good having some strange man saying, "Well, here's your mother after all these years after she abandoned you for the first quarter or so of your life." But do we just forget about that and not have an explanation for those actions? Everilda wanted answers and she was determined to get them.

Astrid took a pause before reciting the next part, the really nitty gritty that would decide whether Everilda could truly handle this revelation or not because it is only when you learn the brutal truth about your heritage that you find out who you are. And Astrid wasn't sure if Everilda was ready for that. I mean, she was barely nineteen years of age. Headstrong. Jealous and impulsive along with a whole list of other qualities that Astrid was exactly certain were a pure match for Rhiannon back in her adolescence.

"Rhiannon was never allowed to be with you due to your father's marriage. And when your father left Damaris, guess who he ran back to? Yep. He and Rhiannon took up together and made their own home in another part of the realm. But until you were eighteen, Rhiannon could not enter your life," Astrid recited carefully before taking another pause as he added in, "But you are almost nineteen years of age now, Everilda. You are not some child that has to be molly coddled and shied away from the world. You can handle anything. Even the truth."

Everilda raised her eyebrows, carefully examining this creature Astrid for anything that she might regard as dodgy or ill-willed but she found he was nothing but honorable. If nothing else, he had better intentions than most people she had met in her life. "I agree," Everilda concurred. "I don't wish to sound rude or ungrateful, but what do you get out of this, telling me about my mother? Filling in the gaps in my sordid family's history?" she asked.

Astrid smirked as he was instantly reminded of Isra. The nonstop questioning. The futile need for answers in which she didn't trust a single one. Oh, my goodness, it was no surprise that these two had ended up as friends, if not only for a little while. The likeness was uncanny and Astrid was beginning to suspect that there was a link here between Isra and Everilda; one that evidently neither of them had any inclination of, whatsoever.

"I get nothing out of it but seeing the smile resounding upon my employer's face for I just reunited mother and daughter after eighteen painful, grueling years," Astrid mustered in a sincere voice as if he really did have faith that what he was doing was just and right. "Also, I solely believe in paying off a debt when one is owed. And so that is why I am here. To reunite you and your mother." Astrid finished much to Everilda's shock who hadn't expected this clearly. "I can take you there but believe me... it might be a rough ride. The place we are going to is known for its hellish reputation," Astrid affirmed, making sure that Everilda understood everything before she agreed to go along with it.

"As if I care about the good and righteous parts of life anymore. Take me there please!" Everilda pleaded but she had a glint in her eye as if there was more to this than she was letting on. For even though Everilda had been cruelly discarded like someone's trash more times than she could care to count, she was always in search of a way to make them pay for their misdeeds.

"Of course. I just wanted you to know the facts before we went. I always believe in paying it forward," Astrid denoted Everilda before he looked out upon the singed grassland that stood around Everilda's home. "Nice place you got here out in the wilderness but I think you'd find a mansion much more to your liking!"

He joked out loud but for some reason Everilda couldn't help but detect a seriousness in his voice like he was making a suggestion to her. In some form or another.

20

Astrid waited patiently at the entrance to the grand stature of a mansion after he had rapped loudly upon the door. It was a monstrosity all right, completely towering over him and Everilda as she too took in the sight before her in awe. Everilda had never seen a place as enormous as this and to think this was her parent's home? It was unfathomable.

She felt as if she was kept here any longer, she'd have to stop to catch her breath. Just the glorious sight of the shapely black building that shone out amongst everything else bemused her. It even contrasted with the skies that were slowly becoming cobalt blue as the queen of the night was on her way to dance alongside the glowing circular moon.

Much to her dismay, a tall man appeared in the doorway. He had black combed-over hair and was dressed in a black silken shirt with matching trousers and also a suit style black overcoat. Obviously, this was Damien Daughtry, Everilda's father, because he eyed the girl carefully before displaying a smirk. However, Astrid initiated the conversation. He certainly didn't want a kerfuffle between Everilda and Damien on the doorstep of all places and certainly not before they'd had a chance to treat others with respect. If such a thing was in existence.

"Good evening, Damien. I have brought you a gift," Astrid announced with a cheery grin.

Finally, having delivered on his promise to Rhiannon, Astrid was nothing but triumphant. He wasn't really family oriented, but this family was almost like his own, since he had known them for years. And for some reason beyond his own recollection Astrid was experiencing joy at having been able to reunite them all, even if things were stiff at best between Damien and his failure of a daughter.

Damien glanced upon Everilda again, giving her the once-over. He didn't smile or display any type of emotion before he moved quickly to address Astrid on the subject. "Aha, this is her? Well, now. Rhiannon will be most pleased with your efforts, Astrid."

He paused as Astrid stood there with Everilda lingering behind him. She felt awkward, needless to say since her father was being so weird with her.

Everilda knew straightaway that this was her father because even though he had not personally introduced himself, she recognized that standoffish energy immediately. It was the very same she had noted from her so-called mother Damaris throughout the years. It was the demeanor that spoke volumes even when the person didn't say a word. It echoed, "Well hey, I don't have a fondness for you, but I'm going to tolerate this by pretending you do not exist on this earth." Yes, it was insufferable to say the least.

He doesn't even like me and yet he's not given me the time of day. Wow. Oh boy, does this sound familiar. It's almost like I'm some discarded piece of excrement on the back of his shoe. This man that is supposedly my father doesn't have the first idea of who I am but yet he's already made up his mind about me.

Astrid was feeling incredibly iffy as he witnessed the standoffish glances between Everilda and Damien. It was more than butterfingers here. The silence between them was deafening and the evil stares were enough to send chills flowing into anybody.

Someone needs to move this hell along. It's not going to be me. Astrid chortled to himself in sardonic thought. *Clearly, I walked into some sheer resentment and I didn't realize how bad it was. Until now.*

"Anyhow, Astrid came in. Please. Rhiannon is sure to be overjoyed," Damien invited Astrid cordially before turning to face his wayward daughter. And finally there seemed to be a glimmer of hope as Damien addressed her warmly, "Oh you too, dear! No doubt a fine cup of coffee will be most pleasurable to your tastes."

It was almost a question but not so as he wasn't actually asking her since he was being so formal.

It was more he was telling her that she'd be enjoying a rich mug of coffee in no time. Or she could indeed leave and find her contentment elsewhere. However, he wasn't verbally saying that to her because well, Damien was far too polite for that. He'd rather be resilient and put on airs than admit that something or someone was bothering him.

DAMIEN LED Everilda and Astrid into his darkened office that had very little light. He came across slightly rude as he didn't offer for either of them to be seated but then Everilda's bold blue eyes caught sight of the bright, blood red hair that dangled from Rhiannon's back. Evidently, she had not noticed Everilda's presence, otherwise there may have been some reaction but it was as though Rhiannon was in the midst of a train of thought as she seemed distracted.

Damien dragged her out of that mind bubble in a second as he called her, "Rhiannon, dear we have guests!"

Rhiannon met her beloved's eyes at once but those same eyes found themselves fleeting upon the glimpse of Everilda. Whatever it was that Rhiannon was preoccupied with was now redundant as she just stared at Everilda. Rhiannon was behaving so intensely that it actually unnerved her daughter a tiny bit, but this was not important. Everilda stood there motionless as her mother for the first time laid eyes on her daughter, a remarkable moment for both dark souls that would never ever be repeated. Rhiannon immediately strode over to Everilda, reaching for her hand and holding it up to heart, clasping it tightly upon her own.

She was emotional as she reached for Everilda's golden hair that hung past her shoulders, twirling the golden blonde strands in her fingers affectionately before gasping, "Oh my goodness. In all my life, I never dreamed you would be so beautiful, child! You amaze me beyond any notion."

Everilda was silent, not knowing how to respond but when you compared that she had been more or less insulted all her life, this was likely her first ever endearing compliment and it had come from the woman that had made her no less. She couldn't help but burst into a beaming smile at which Rhiannon hugged Everilda, pulling her up against her chest, holding her tightly. "All these years, girl. We have so much to catch up on," Rhiannon mustered with glee.

Astrid saw the scene before him and not wanting to intrude, he glanced at Rhiannon and muttered gladly, "I shall leave you two to it. You have much to discuss."

But just as he turned to leave Rhiannon undertook it upon herself to thank him. She was overwhelmed by his generosity. It wasn't often that someone kept their end of the bargain and for that she was most indebted to him.

"Oh, Astrid! I cannot thank you enough for what you have done in bringing my daughter to me. Without you, we'd have never had this precious time together," Rhiannon expressed with ripened emotion as she rested her palm on Everilda's head affectionately touching her golden blonde hair.

"The pleasure was all mine. I have a date with a certain femme fatale so while I wish I could stay, I have other places to be," Astrid recited with a triumphant smile as he walked away, bowing to Damien on his way out.

He was on his way straight to Isra because where else would he be? He'd done his duty. Delivered on what he had promised and so now he had new pastures to explore but before he could leave, Damien signaled a warning finger at Astrid, telling him that he was going to have a swift quiet word with him before he made his departure.

"Astrid, I have something for you, something to help you on your quest," Damien offered in a cheery tone. "Call it my humble gratitude," Damien muttered before he whispered something in Astrid's ear.

It was unknown what words were spoken but the confident grin that resounded upon Astrid's face as Damien handed him a well concealed object was enough to conclude that whatever it was something very helpful to his wondrously anarchic cause.

21

Astrid charged down to Shambre Fell fast as fire, not stopping until he reached those glorious aquamarine hues with a sparkling gleam that came off the long-running stream that guarded the area in question. And then of course there was the majestic tower that stood in amongst the land, making everything else around it look invariably small, just like ants as the magnificent chateau stood triumphant above all else. Astrid thought if he hurried he could get there in time because surely Isra was going to be there. She had no business being at Wingdom's Academy now and with Everilda reunited with her parents at Sprawnbell, there was nothing to keep Isra there. Isra didn't have any knowledge of such an event as yet, but give it time because good things always come to those who wait.

Sprinting ahead plundering through the grass bank just beyond the stream, Astrid finally got his view of the picturesque realm that he hoped he would find Isra in. He was banking everything on finding her here because where else would she honestly be?

He could have tried going off to Glamvein but they had used that location so many times now for their meetings that it was starting to become routine. Astrid didn't like routine and neither did he like being predictable. That meant that if Glamvein was his and Isra's most treasured spot to rendezvous then just about anyone could scope them out there. Astrid could not have that! He'd much rather they'd have somewhere secluded in which to commune.

However, if Astrid was going to continue making progress with her then efforts would have to be doubled because Astrid was just seeing a glimmer of the rose bushes that lay dormant by the entrance to Shambre Fell. There was something there, a light shadow highlighted by the end of the galley where the rose bushes stood in a line. Just the faint flicker of a shimmery yellow bubble floating out of nowhere. It was pretentious but as Astrid strode closer to the roses, he was sure it was Isra. Maybe it was wishful thinking, but Astrid persevered as he got nearer to the yellowy golden light hovering around the rose bushes.

The light took on a life of its own as that white golden head reared upward revealing a pair of piercing lime green eyes of which there could only be one owner. Yes, it was Isra. She had been fumbling around with the foliage, tending to the roses and delicately replanting some loose stray roots into the soil as though they were her children, being careful not to break off any of the fragile greenery as she submitted it back down into its natural habitat.

It was looking to Astrid as if Isra really would be living in Shambre Fell and much sooner than he had anticipated. He couldn't resist giving Isra a comedic grin as though he had been expecting this. He narrowed his big bright yellow golden eyes at her but gave her that beaming smile like he was pleased to see her. And of course, he was, so there was no deceitful intent being portrayed by him because he was absolutely delighted to see her.

Isra responded by flashing him an icy cold stare, one that was met with nervousness as she gave what resembled a smile but not quite so. More like a glare but that tiny bit of smile could be detected underneath the facade she put on.

"I didn't think anybody would find me here!" Isra announced under her breath as she didn't even look at Astrid. She kept her eyes on the purple rose bush she had been pruning and re rooting as if her life had depended upon it. Some part of Isra didn't want to face Astrid because maybe him coming out here to find her just before nightfall had been exactly what she had been wanting, although she wasn't going to be caught admitting that notion.

"Oh really?" he pressed with a wide-eyed grin. A smirk appearing on the side of his face indicated he had rumbled her little white lie but was he honestly going to call her out on it. "Ha, now girl. You knew I would come back here! We are aligned far more than you care to acknowledge but enough of that. I think you and I should go somewhere a little less populated for I have a proposition for you," Astrid announced in a low voice although by how brash he was being, he definitely meant what he was saying.

Isra looked taken back. Her lime green eyes fell upon him immediately in a razor-sharp stare met with curiosity. "A proposition for me?? And what would that entail?" Isra probed. She was skeptical since he was just jumping out with this ideal out of nowhere. Like he had plucked it out of his hat or something but maybe there was more behind it than she had dared to notice.

"Yes, well..." Astrid trailed off. He put his index finger to his lips, thinking deeply about the matter at hand. If he was going to do this right it would have to be somewhere really cut off from the rest of the world. *A wasteland, perhaps?* Astrid communed to himself in thought. *Or maybe that grand pasture is just not too far away from Spirisity?? It needs to be somewhere complacent that is idle. Away from prying eyes, most importantly. Oh, I know, I'll take her to Nefaria Sands. The sinned yellow singed land that no one dares to tread upon for fear they might sink into the deadly chilled waters that barricade it from everybody else. Samuel and company won't think of going there. Oh no, I'll get to have my devilish fun without any rude interruptions.*

Finally, Astrid had a smile on his face as he now had confirmation on exactly where to go. "I know of a place. But it's bitterly cold unless you have a well-adjusted body like mine that can adapt to just about any temperature or climate," Astrid retorted dryly as he took note of Isra's facial expressions.

He was judging her on her resilience that she had exhibited with him before, he predicted that she could be difficult to sway but he wasn't going to be thwarted so easily. It was true that she had warmed to him a little. Perhaps becoming lukewarm instead of frosty like she had been on their very first face to face meeting.

"And how would we get to such a place with fearfully cold waters?" Isra inquired with a furrowed brow.

The way her eyes met Astrid's with such idle curiosity only gave him more motivation as he found himself looking at such an innocent soul with those bright lime green eyes. A childlike fondness and a yearning to know things that could only endeavor to make Astrid smile because for all her darkness and icy cold demeanor she still had that spark in her. That distinctive but admirable imagination that only certain souls had the ability to possess.

"Funny you ask that!" Astrid smiled at her before he reached for her hand in preparation for his next action in which Isra would indeed see just how they would arrive at their destination.

Isra hesitated for a second before placing her hand into Astrid's. He wasn't lying about having a strange way with temperatures. His skin was red hot to the touch but as though he was a fierce open furnace. Or maybe he had simply walked on hot coals. Either way, Astrid was hot as hell to Isra. Literally.

"Don't you trust me? Come now, after everything we've been through, girl!" Astrid retorted in a sarcastic tone but yet he wasn't angry as he was still smiling. Also, he found much amusement in the situation as he gave a little smirk here and there, indicating that he was being incredibly lighthearted about it all.

"Well. It's not that I don't, it's just you are still a stranger," Isra mouthed in a meek tone. She didn't want to become complacent or sound apathetic like she needed this man to validate her or something like that.

"Nonsense!" Astrid recalled to her. "Not after I gave you the sacred creed that James and Samuel were keeping from you. I'm the only one who has been wholly truthful with you."

Astrid didn't give Isra an inch. He didn't want to take the risk that she might slip away from him again. And knowing her, she was just pacing herself for the perfect opportunity to do just that so without delay, he hastily clicked his thumb and forefinger together and the next thing he knew, he was staring at bright turquoise ocean seas.

~

Isra put her hand over her mouth in awe of where she was. Removing the urge to gasp, she feasted her eyes on the site before her. Perhaps it was just an abandoned island or a world that had been long forgotten timeless eons ago, but Isra found herself bewitched as she stood next to Astrid transfixed by the beautiful majesty that surrounded her.

It was impossible to ignore the frosty turquoise hues that were peeking out in between translucent shimmery white as waves came crashing in against the bitter lemon yellow sands only told her she was in a place truly wondrous. It was evidently somewhere the naked eye could not take in and likely a location you only find yourself in if you were metaphysically capable of mastering such a feat.

Resisting the inclination to force her hand out of Astrid's, yanking it out of his palm, Isra could only marvel at what she was being exposed to. "Wow. This is absolutely beautiful, Astrid," she gasped, still shocked at the beauty of such an island for she had never seen it before, ever in her entire existence.

"It's stunning isn't it?" Astrid agreed. "It's really truly something you would only expect to find in a subliminal dream."

"Yes. It really is. But why did you bring me here?" Isra asked him meticulously. She was idly wondering as to why he'd take her so far out of the land and have this magnificence wash over her. Although as transfixing as it was, there must have been a reason for it.

"Aha! I cannot hide anything from you for long, can I?" Astrid chuckled before retaining his serious flair as he stared at Isra intently knowing that she was already onto him.

"No, you cannot," Isra replied with an amused tone, "But it is most sweet in how you try, dear."

Isra flashed him a smile. It was as if she was already suspecting there was more in the bargain than she had anticipated. This Astrid fellow wasn't really one to reveal too much of himself. Even to her.

"Very well, then," Astrid remarked before lifting out a glowing green round globe of what appeared to be magic. It was sparkling and gleaming, flashing angry glares as it hissed and sizzled while lying dormant in Astrid's hand. "Do you remember a certain light bringer taking this beautiful commodity away from you?" Astrid asked her plainly.

Isra gasped at the sight of the round glowing orb that Astrid held warmly in his hand. It was bright effervescent lime green magic. She'd recognized it from anywhere. Isra had fondly remembered creating that just after she had summoned Franco or maybe it was before. She couldn't recollect the exact details but she did recall conjuring up the bewitching green robust entity.

"Yes," she mustered, unable to conceive the notion that Astrid had managed to reclaim the magic she had believed to be lost to her because Samuel had made it seem like it had been obliterated.

Astrid lowered his eyes at her closely in an attempt of deliberation to disclose to her just how he had mastered such a dishonorable feat. "A dear friend of mine retrieved this from Samuel's very own supposedly locked down office. Now I am handing it back to you. Isra, I believe you can do some great things. You have power in you. I'd like to be the one that sets you on your path. If only you can do the great honor of seeing my vision of you coming unto reality." Astrid finished before extending his hand forward, presenting the glowing green orb to Isra. He was hoping she would accept it from him.

She has to take it from me. Isra is so young and there is still so much she has to learn but I believe she has the presence and ability to truly set the world on fire, Astrid elaborated to himself in thought.

"Yes, you have said so many times," Isra replied, unable to take her eyes off the glowing green orb. This fascinating, sparkly being was calling to her, sending all manner of chaotic mesmerizing energy her way as it howled at her in its own unique way.

"And I mean every word," Astrid affirmed clearly to her. He

wasted no time now. They had been standing here for long enough. It was time to get right down to it. She'd had this tempting prize alluring her from afar, keeping her eyes bejeweled by its beauty. Astrid wanted to see if Isra was going to be receptive when it came down to the destructive energies that she possessed inside herself. Really, Astrid yearned to know if Isra deemed herself worthy of such a gleaming spectacle.

Astrid handed the green glowing orb of magic to Isra. It was odd to Isra as she did not hesitate. Not for a moment. Isra gratefully reached her hand over to the powerful orb in Astrid's hand, allowing her hand to touch his own as her fingers hovered above it just gently feeling out it's fiery energy before she took a deep breath, taking hold of it.

Only too happy to oblige in her cause for greatness, Astrid let Isra grab the glowing ball with both hands, allowing it to be lifted off his palm as Isra found it bemusing her as she just stared into it. Astrid couldn't help but smile as she did so. Finally, she was administering some control in her life. Doing something that benefited herself for the very first time. Nobody would be able to steal this from her. She had well and truly earned it.

Obviously Isra hadn't noticed the gratified look on Astrid's face, otherwise she might have pulled her hand away but he was proud of the woman she had become. Even if she didn't know it. Isra clasped onto the round green globe of magic with her dominant hand, looking back as it singed and sparkled with fury as she held it. Feeling triumphant, Astrid turned toward Isra's face as she still held the power entity in her hand but then a familiar face appeared in front of Astrid, startling him.

Those sky-blue eyes were unmistakable. Not to mention the jet-black combed back hair that framed his only too perfect face. A furrowed brow that met Astrid's golden yellow eyes with a serious glare only cemented Astrid's worst fears. Oh yes, it was the superior master of the universe himself. And he'd got here just in the nick of time by the look of it. Evidently the light bringer was perturbed at

Astrid since he was brandishing Astrid with a stone burning glare as though he was not best pleased with Astrid.

However, Astrid wasn't going to let that spoil anything. Astrid could only send a beseeching evil stare back at his once so fondly looked upon employer. And he very much doubted he wasn't putting too much faith into the past tense for after this Samuel was sure to send him on his heels.

"Samuel," Astrid mustered with a sardonic tone. The vile emitted off his voice was enough to suggest that Astrid wasn't overjoyed by Samuel's appearance either.

"Astrid," Samuel mouthed back at Astrid. Samuel folded his arms pressing them against his chest in an irritated stance. "How did I know I'd find you here with the princess of darkness?" he retorted sarcastically, keeping his arms crossed but his eyes were on both Astrid and Isra as though both of them were in a lot of hot water.

Samuel posed the pressing inquiry but it wasn't really a question. More a statement but it told Astrid all that he needed to know, that James had been swift in telling Samuel all as Astrid had always suspected he would.

"James squealed then?" Astrid countered with a vexed expression.

"Yes. Yes, he did. And a good thing too, because here you are about to unleash Armageddon unto the world with our little spitfire!" Samuel muttered before he turned his focus to Isra.

Samuel gave Isra a warm smile for he didn't want to show any animosity despite the fact that she was holding a most powerful forcefulness in her right hand and that at any point, she could use that to destroy everything in sight.

"Oh my girl, you are in more trouble than you can believe right now. But it's still not too late even after all this..."

Samuel motioned to her as he pointed at the scene around them. Astrid still stood next to Isra, almost guarding her in a sense. Isra stood motionless as she still held the green orb in her hand but kept looking back at Samuel as if she had no inclination of what was going to happen next.

"It isn't?" Isra questioned Samuel. "But then, didn't you always believe it was too late for me? After all, you had me down as some sort of queen of the night!" Isra retorted in Samuel's direction.

Samuel did nothing but give Isra a firm warning glance as she looked around at him before finally eyeing up Astrid, of whom did little for her knowledge seeking as he didn't know where to look. It was as though Isra was seeking validation that all of this was correct, that she was really here on this lonely, deserted island with these two men and everything was about to tumble.

"Aha, so he did tell you! That is accurate; we always pertained to you in that way but it doesn't change what you have been enlisted to do here. You know, Astrid is a very stubborn soul and what he has told you is indeed true, but you don't know the half of it, my dear," Samuel replied in an earnest tone before he lowered his voice, softening Isra up before reciting gently but firmly, "So please, save me from doing something I will not regret because believe me, girl, I have the means to stop you. I will stop you if I am forced to do so."

Isra's eyes heightened at the thought of it. This bold, brave man Samuel was willing to risk it all in halting her before she could do a thing and yet here was Astrid. Astrid was a very courageous soul despite his cocky wit and lack of finery but he had been the one that had led her to this moment. Astrid had made Isra see herself and oddly enough, she was okay with the vision that looked back at her. A notion she had never imagined she would believe in. But it was justly so and that further impacted her admiration of the man Astrid even though she had barely begun to know him.

Ultimately she would have to make a choice as to which leader to follow. Would it be Samuel with his sweet talking of her to make her stop, or would it be Astrid the one who had encouraged her to be who she wanted all along? Her choice would not be easy but Isra had already decided on whom she was going to act upon.

Turning to Samuel before winking at Astrid, Isra had Samuel's full attention as she motioned, "I'm sorry, but it's going to be Astrid that I follow."

Samuel unfolded his arms as he addressed Isra before making his approach to her which only made Astrid uneasy but even Astrid had no comprehension of what was coming. "As I had presumed. Very well," Samuel responded curtly.

Astrid could only quiver as Samuel stepped behind Isra. First of all, he walked around her in a complete circle before he covered her mouth with his hand. This caused Isra to shudder in amazement for she had no clue what was happening but Samuel had been prepared for this moment from the very first time he had ever laid eyes on her.

"This will only hurt for a moment. I promise," Samuel whispered into her ear while he still had his hand blocking her from speaking.

And it was with this that Samuel took the glowing green orb from Isra's dominant hand before snatching it up into his own free hand then crushing it to smithereens in an instant. There it went into oblivion. It was at this point that Samuel took his hand away from Isra's mouth so that she was free to speak again. Isra immediately tried to run away from her position in the sand, only to find that her feet appeared to be rooted deep within the earth, still noting that Samuel was behind her. Isra realized she was transfixed into this almost meditative state where she barely heard anything but Samuel's soothing voice.

Samuel was only too happy to coax Isra into a deeper state of being as he allowed his next part of his plan to unfold. By putting her arms behind her back and holding them there for a second with his left hand, Samuel affixed Isra to this space so she could not break free while he stayed behind her. "Calm yourself. I told you I would disarm you!" Samuel commanded as he whispered into her ear once more.

Samuel placed his palm on Isra's third eye, just below her forehead and a fiery silver light sparkling like glowing embers of gold showered Isra, Astrid, and Samuel, immediately covering them in the radiant warmth of the light. Silvery light tumbled down from the heavens washing over Isra from head to foot until it was totally diminished and Isra was left looking back at both him and Astrid in bemusement.

Astrid could only watch in awe as Samuel motioned to him. "Oh boy, I bet you wish you'd done something different than this, huh? Don't worry; she won't remember anything for as long as you both live in my eternity. The light always has a way of conquering the dark. She won't know who you are and neither will she have any memory of you and her ever conversing. Or these happenings," Samuel said with a sharp twang in his voice as though he was annoyed but yet pleased with himself.

The sheer magnitude of the magic that Samuel had just enacted was revealed when Samuel lifted his hand away from her forehead and Isra spun her head around in shock. She was dazed and confused, bringing her hands to her forehead feeling an icy cold burn on her head but not having any idea as to how it had gotten there. Isra was wondering where on earth she was as her eyes flitted from side to side as it was apparent to her that Samuel and Astrid were strangers.

Astrid resisted the need to call to her, to sound out her name but it was already certain that Isra had no recollection of who he was. Samuel had done a pristine job in wiping her memory clean and now Isra was standing in the sand, looking back at both Samuel and Astrid for some answers.

However, Samuel wasn't about to give her any and all it took was a simple wave of his hand and Isra disappeared in a ray of golden light. As to where, Astrid didn't have any inclination of but knowing Samuel, it was likely in a place Astrid would never find her again. But before Astrid could let the realization that he had lost Isra for good sink in, Samuel waved his hand again. This action took Astrid from a robust humanized form to black silken feathers as he was lowered onto the ground, staring back at himself in the sea's reflection.

Samuel hadn't just taken away Isra and her memories, but he'd also made sure that Astrid would have very little chance of doing the same thing with her again.

22

Samuel straightened himself, arching his back to get more comfortable as he sat in his favorite red velvet armchair while a steaming hot mug of coffee was situated next to him on his solid wooden desk.

Astrid could only glance upwards at the light bringer as he perched a couple of feet away on one of the idle chairs that were positioned parallel to Samuel's desk while they also gave a grand view of the world outside showcasing Spirisity proudly while also displaying the other beautiful facets of the land. Astrid was sore in his heart, having lost Isra when Samuel intervened only an hour ago and now was the dreaded talk, the one where he and Samuel would come face to face and finally discuss all that had been bothering Astrid. It was the conversation that would also establish why Astrid had rebelled so much against Samuel's wishes although honestly, Astrid really didn't want to have it.

He'd had enough; feeling defeated as he'd had to watch Samuel take Isra's precious memories away from her, making Astrid a stranger to her as he swept her entire head clean of everything. Meeting Astrid. The moment where Astrid had detailed to her of the prophecy surrounding her and even the final moment they'd had together where Astrid had handed Isra some of the greatest power she could ever hope to own. But of course, now all of that is gone, courtesy of Samuel. So it was only natural Astrid would harbor some resentment toward Samuel, but Samuel didn't care for that.

"Astrid," Samuel finally mouthed after what seemed like centuries of Astrid being alone, secluded in his gathering thoughts of the events of that day.

"Samuel..." Astrid replied. His tone was musty yet formal for he was showing no emotion, just a blank canvas as though this was a business meeting of sorts. Astrid wasn't about to show just how downtrodden he really felt.

Samuel narrowed his eyes at Astrid carefully before he remarked in an earnest tone, "I know you are probably very irked by me right now, but I had no choice, boy. You and Isra were in far too deep. I had to step in."

Samuel turned to the window that showed the paradise of Spirisity in all its glory. Acres of green grassy land surrounded by soft green hills amongst a crystal-clear blue sky stood out like a painting.

Samuel couldn't help but admire the view as he retorted to Astrid honestly. "You know in the scheme of things, I knew you were going to end up with her. I just hadn't realized how far you'd gone down. You used to be so much more, Astrid. You had a passion for the work we did in bringing those darkened back to the light but with this girl, woman, whatever she was. You were besotted from the start and I knew there on, that you would only plunder further until it was at such a point that neither of you could return from such a state of extremity."

"Honestly, boy. I knew there were destructive traits in you and perhaps it was my fault since I disregarded them, but I had always been good to you. I had always taken care of you, ensuring you were understanding of the matters at hand and that there was no indifference. Although you going to Damien Daughtry and getting transformed into a human was never on my radar. But I had so many hopes for you. I guess in the end you disappointed me but I always knew deep in the back of my mind that you always would so I can't scold you too much for that," Samuel retorted candidly.

Astrid said nothing. He didn't really know what he could say that would change any of this. He could only meet Samuel's blue glinting eyes with his own yellow ones and feel the harsh branding that was coming down upon him.

Samuel continued whilst still gazing out of the window onto the majestic land in front of his eyes. "I feel there is nothing left here for you, Astrid. I have done all I can to be a strong fatherly figure to you and it's simply not been enough."

Astrid still wasn't sure on what he should say and so he dropped his head down to his claws before agreeing with Samuel. "You are right, master. But I'd do it again. I know you don't understand my reasoning as to why. I was so drawn to Isra from the moment I heard her name and even her wretched origins. I was delighted by the glow in her eyes even when she was weeping beside me. She was unlike anything I had ever known. I'd risk it all over and over again just to get a glimpse of her," Astrid blurted out, realizing he'd had actually admitted his feelings for her unknowingly.

This made Samuel take his focus away from the glorious sights outside, turning to Astrid with a furrowed brow as though something was troubling him. It was clear to Astrid that there was something that sounded very final in Samuel's voice as though this was a culmination between them both.

"It's not what I wanted to hear Astrid, but I thank you for your honesty. Perhaps we can let the matter settle for a few days and then attempt to get back to normality. Whatever that is," Samuel concurred.

"And Isra?" Astrid piped up. He didn't want to sound too eager but he was desperate to know what had become of her even though he doubted that he'd ever see her again.

"She's safe. Out of harm's way, but will always be watched by the closeness of Spirisity. You could say she's still our little pet project but it doesn't change anything, Astrid. She has no memory of knowing you. I know that must sting but it really is for the better end of both of you. Even if you cannot see beyond that for now," Samuel finished sharply.

"It really is for the best, boy. You two were too dangerous to exist together as one. Someone had to put an end to it. People just don't understand that sometimes love can be our own worst enemy because two souls are sometimes so well matched for each other that all their dark and evil characteristics can only clash in a fiery blaze amongst the good. It is that way even if we choose to overlook that tiny detail," Samuel mustered before he turned away to the window again, having had no more to say to Astrid.

As far as Samuel was concerned, this was it.

23

-One year later-

Dawn had arrived. A warm glow emitted from the sky. The golden rays gently glided across the land to launch in the day.

A raven drifted in and out of the white fluffy clouds, bright eyed and buzzing with energy. His black wings were dazzling and shiny as they glided in the morning light. The raven swooped down, hovering above the luscious landscape before him, a blur of yellow and green pasture. Sunny crocuses poked their tiny heads out amongst the grassy meadow decorated by sweet violets. The quaint little was garden tucked away in the outskirts of a wilderness

The raven scanned the area carefully, keeping his eyes peeled for a gray castle. That was his reason for coming here, although he couldn't see anything resembling a castle near him. Hmmm, he'd have to keep searching, for it must be somewhere around here. He slowed himself to get a clearer view. His citrine eyes glowed as he flew lower, getting closer to the amber colored terrain. One eye was fixed on the lime meadow abreast with floral flavor while the other looked around and ahead of him.

Behind this exquisite garden were acres of highland hills covered in the finest fern green grass. As he veered closer towards the hills, he caught sight of a tall building a horrid, dull gray color.

The raven smiled. This place was barely accessible and hidden away from the world. He flew over, swiftly landing on the soft grass making a quiet landing. He maneuvered himself to the door, grasping the handle with his beak, willing it to fly open. He entered the castle, observing the decadent walls in pomegranate finished with gilded gold framing were just like they were, the last time he was here. He gracefully climbed the golden staircase to the top floor.

The raven used his beak to push past a royal blue curtain, giving him entry in the room that was hidden behind it. A red cushioned chair rested against the midnight blue wall. Upon the chair reading an old, tattered book was a man. He had black hair, short but slicked back at the front but long enough to cover the base of his forehead. Moon-shaped glasses hung off his nose as he peeked at the raven with intrigued fascination.

"So, you're back, Astrid?" Samuel inquired. A wistful look of curiosity was in his eye. He closed the book with his right hand, placing it on the window ledge beside him.

"Yes!" Astrid cawed. He swerved over to the red chair, sitting beside Samuel. A sense of admiration could be noticed as he joyfully stood on his claws.

"And what did you learn?" Samuel asked, placing a finger on his lip, awaiting some tasty diligent detail that he wasn't sure he wanted to hear. But still he pressed on with his line of questioning. It was important to him.

Samuel worried about Astrid, the young raven, for he was a reckless soul, rebelling against what society deemed he must do and choosing his own path. That path was quite often the dark one, a way of living that was frowned upon for a raven to be undertaking. Astrid was no exception to this as he often found himself placated into things he could not get out of. He got himself way too deep of a dark hole more than once and someone would have to retrieve him back into the lighter way of being. In fact, it was only one year ago that

Samuel had to step in to pull Astrid out of another mess. One that involved a very well-known witch, who was soon to be known as Lady Isra of the Dark. She had been fondly named so because of the prophecies pertaining to her.

Astrid, despite his misdemeanors, had been taught wisely by those closest to him the secrets of living a happy life. Samuel was Astrid's master and friend. Samuel had been accommodating to Astrid's every need and whim since he had found the raven lurking about his castle with the news that he had no habitual home or friends he could rely on. He was a loner raven which Samuel found riveting as he had presumed ravens swarmed together in groups.

How wrong he was.

Samuel was concerned for Astrid because he had been acting distant in recent times, not his usual self as he would go gallivanting out into the night without a second word to Samuel, nor did he ask permission before leaving.

Astrid cleared his throat before blurting, "The young witch Isra has come of age. She is nineteen years old now."

Samuel smiled, for he knew what was coming next. Forbidden fruit came to mind. Something so deadly that it would be perilous to anyone that went near it. In this case, it was a female. "Yes, she has," Samuel agreed. He wasn't going to argue over the facts. He paused before submitting, "But she's rooted in dark forces. She's covered in them by her own inception. They rush over her like warm blood flowing over a corpse." Samuel knew that this wasn't going to go down well.

"I disagree," Astrid concurred. "There could still be a chance. I'd like to help her..." he said quietly, trailing off. *If she'd accept my help,* he murmured quietly to himself.

Samuel glared at Astrid although his look was warm and caring. "Do you think someone as ghastly as Lady Isra of the Dark wants assistance? Especially coming from a light bearer such as yourself?"

Astrid shrugged that off. Even someone truly dark and embodied in evil can still want help at some point in her life.

"She hasn't inherited that title Lady Isra of the Dark yet," Astrid asserted, looking toward Samuel.

Samuel's sky-blue eyes were affixed onto Astrid's in a stern frown. "But she will. The prophecy said she'd turn her own heart inside out, ripping it from her own chest. Inviting in the darkness. You saw her rip her heart out for yourself. Don't deny that you saw it because you know it is true. Of course, I understand that you'd rather circumstances had turned out differently," Samuel added at the last second.

While he was going to be sullen with Astrid, he certainly didn't want to harm the young raven's feelings. He'd had an interest in the young sorceress Isra since he had laid eyes on her. Samuel knew this wasn't just some idle crush and he wasn't some hapless teenager. Astrid clearly had set his sights on her but those same sights had got the raven in a lot of hot water and that was only a year ago. Samuel couldn't help but feel Astrid was backing a losing horse, so to speak, as light beings and dark forces rarely collaborated as one.

Astrid piped up eagerly. "I don't feel she is as ghastly as you phrase it. I feel she is one that has gone into the lands of the dark with the ideal that she can shy away from all good. I believe there is potential in her. I won't lose hope."

Samuel paused and smiled before saying, "She has no memory of who you are. But if you insist on going about this cause, you would have to start from the very beginning, gaining her trust just like James did."

Astrid seemed annoyed by that as he responded, "But James was a mere mortal, not even anything more than human. Although I have to say he never smelled human. My point is, Isra didn't really take to him that well. I'm more of a resounding match for her interminable soulless being." Astrid gloated a little more than he had expected to be.

Samuel eyed Astrid once more, chuckling as he recited, "James was only following my orders. Him and I set this up from the very beginning, but of course you knew that. You had prowess of your own. You managed to conquer everything we had to block you from getting to her and just to even the scales, you unleashed some of your own. It doesn't surprise me that you two are likely a good vibrational match despite the negatives that reside in you both. For you and Isra are one of the same."

Samuel took a small pause before continuing, "I'm not stupid, I know how you are going to play this. It has come to my attention that this is your sole wish. So, I must honor it, but first I have to banish you from the land. You are to never return, Astrid; do you hear me?" Samuel barked although his tone was merely formal considering he was sending Astrid away from his employment forever.

However, Samuel wasn't as cold as he was appearing to be when he turned his eyes to Astrid once more, almost smiling at him before saying, "This is my final parting gift to you. Her heart is rooted in darkness, that is for sure but one day she will open her heart to another again. I have no idea if it will be you or another man, but he will be her ultimate confidant. Isra will want this companion to be with her until the very day that her immortality expires, for then her humanity will rise again."

ASTRID DEPARTED from Spirisity that very same day, perplexed about that final meeting and those words that had come out of Samuel's mouth, something very odd detailing that Isra would once again be human. But how could such a thing be possible since she was an immortal witch? Astrid didn't understand it but that didn't matter, for he was on a course of self-fulfillment, seeking out knowledge like any other soul destined for greatness that had been clouded by much darkness. He was in flight and almost at his destination; a gray spindling tower appeared in his vision. It rose high up into the hemisphere standing out amongst the pink and orange cloudless skies.

Astrid slowed himself as he came closer and closer to the tower that was fondly called as Shambre Fell. Of course, it was no surprise since Samuel had fabricated this land out of nothingness that he had gave it an endearing name while also placing the subject of Astrid's affections, Isra, here. It was funny as Samuel had told Astrid that he'd never find Isra but that she was safe from any danger while also being kept watched by the soulful beings that heralded from Spirisity but Astrid had never believed that. He'd never given up hope of finding her again.

It had taken a lot of mental toil and going within himself in meditation to discover the truth of what really was. Once Astrid was in a better place emotionally, healing from his loss while also growing spiritually, it was then that he had remembered the iconic land of Shambre Fell that Samuel had planned for Isra to reside in.

Back when he and Isra were carrying on, almost about to wreak havoc unto the world, Astrid had recalled a memory where he had seen Isra tending to a purple rose in the gardens of Shambre Fell. He had remembered thinking that she was probably going to end up here very soon, although Isra never admitted it at the time. But Astrid had gone back into his memory, into that sacred realm within himself where he could commune with Isra at any time he pleased and every time he went there to connect with her, he would always find her in Shambre Fell so it was only natural for Astrid to assume that was her place of residency. Although Astrid had not caught sight of Isra for a year, he was banking all on faith that this was indeed the place he'd find her.

He narrowed his eyes further down as he came to an upstairs window at the top of the tower. This had to be it. It looked like the very same that was home to the upstairs bedroom. Astrid maneuvered himself so that he was situated right outside that window. Gently landing on the stone ledge, he turned himself around, peaking beyond the transparent glass guarded by an iron frame.

There inside was an ornate poster bed about four-feet high with ruby red silk curtains surrounding the bed itself that was covered in white and red sheets. Amongst all the blood red and the icy white, Astrid noticed golden ringlets hanging down from a silken white pillow. The ringlets belonged to a figure sleeping on the white sheets.

The hair dropped down to her bosom and although her eyes were closed, Astrid could see even from afar that this was indeed Isra. Oh my, Samuel had gone as far to place Isra in the very same place he had wanted her to be in all along. How fanciful that he'd said to Astrid that she was in a location that he'd never find her when she'd been under his beak the whole time.

As beautiful as she was with her long golden hair trailing down her slender body with a shiny white negligee dress that contrasted with the bedding, seeing Isra was far too painful for Astrid as he knew he couldn't be with her, not just yet. So, shedding a tear, he looked at her one last time.

"One day I will come back to you. I promise. We will begin anew, and you will fall in love with me all over again."

The End.

DARK SPELL SERIES READING ORDER

1. Her Dark Love
2. Kissing Darkness
3. Seducing Darkness
4. Queen of Darkness
5. Her Dark Soul
6. Her Dark Heart
7. Her Dark Rose
8. Darkness Reborn

ABOUT THE AUTHOR

USA Today Best Seller Isra Sravenheart resides in the UK. She is an avid reader, particularly in the fantasy and paranormal genres, and very much into all things fairytale and dark in nature. She is also a witty wordsmith.

Isra is known for being obsessed with coffee and very particular towards cats of which she owns four of the buggers.

You can follow Isra through her blog, or any of these social media platforms:

ALSO BY ISRA SRAVENHEART

The Dark Spell Series: Books 1 through 8

Heart of Oz

Tainted Siren

The Divine Spiritual Truth: A Twinflame Romance